The Molotov Cocktail

Prize Winners Anthology

Vol. 6

Edited by Josh Goller

Portland, Oregon
USA

themolotovcocktail.com

Editor: Josh Goller
Associate Editor: Mary Lenoir Bond

ISBN: 978-1-7368579-1-5

Contents

Odyssey:

Monsters

"What would an ocean be without a monster lurking in the dark? It would be like sleep without dreams."

– Werner Herzog

Dead Man from the Ocean Floor

by Neil Clark

He climbed into my boat tonight, seawater spewing from the bottoms of his trouser legs, a thousand tiny crabs crawling in and out the holes in his bloated, blue flesh.

When I was young and the things under my bed reached up and stroked the soles of my feet, I survived by befriending them.

So, I offered this man some supper. Tried to make conversation.

I could have sworn I boiled the potatoes in fresh water, but they came out salty as hell. The cured meat bloomed with sea fleas. The plate was a haunted rock pool, the base a spectral, rusty green.

Between ravenous mouthfuls, he told me the ocean had taken him quietly in his sleep. Treated him like the sky might treat an angel.

You give yourself to the marine life, he said. You make your peace with thoughts of your family saying their goodbyes to an empty casket. You just hope that one day some regurgitated fraction of you will end up in a grain of sand between their toes as they sit on a beach somewhere, watching the waves lap the shore, hoping whatever happened to you out here happened painlessly.

We drank brine and talked about childhood nights with the things from under the bed. Letting blood-sucking vampires win at solitaire. Distracting killer clowns with Game Boy. Humming soft lullabies to weeping ghosts. Trying so hard not to cry too loud and wake the ones in the next room and make things so much worse.

Rotting fish roe seeped from his tear ducts, popping and trickling down to the corners of his mouth. Just like in the bedroom, his sobs were silent.

Outside, the storm roared on. Waves punched the hull like missiles.

His trousers did not stop gushing all over the cabin, the flow getting heavier and heavier and the water changing from clear and bitter cold to light brown to boiling deep red.

He dipped his hand into the rising liquid. Algae clung to his exposed bones. He touched my forehead and lowered his skeletal fingers down past my nose. They smelled of the metallic tang in your nostrils when a blast of fluid surges up.

He stroked my arm and led me to the massive rip in the side of the boat. I saw every crystal of salt in the ocean, clear as individual stars.

The waves around us slowed, like sniveling breaths after a fever dream, a peaceful sleep finally washing over.

Will it hurt when my lungs explode? I asked.

Relax, he said. They already have.

#

Neil Clark is the speck of sawdust inside the smallest figure in a lost set of Russian dolls. He thinks about the stars, often.

Happy Is He

by Christina Harrington

Mister Fish took little Gracie Ash from her bed and ate her up like a communion wafer. Placed thin strips of her flesh upon his old, grey tongue and melted her away, until she was cozy inside of his belly, with his ribs for a pillow.

Momma says if I track in mud from the yard one more time, Mister Fish will come for me. But my older brother Charlie tells me Mister Fish will get me no matter what I do. Charlie pinches my arms and the skin along my side and calls me Billy Babyfat.

"How your fat will pop and sizzle," Charlie says. "It'll smoke up his hut!"

I do not look at Mister Fish when we pass him on the street. I keep my eyes upon the stones, the mud caught between them. I have only seen his boots. Charlie tells me he is grey, even his skin, that he has a long, greasy mustache, silver as the rest of him. He says Mister Fish has grey eyes, too, small and bulging, like spider eggs. He smiles at everyone.

Mister Fish smiled when they hung him the first time. Everyone knows that. He smiled at the end of that rope, and his corpse smiled all while they buried him in potter's field, beside the orchard. He smiled, still, when the owner of the cider mill found him the next morning among the twisted apple trees and the fog, noose still tight around his neck, teeth flecked with red apple flesh.

"He smiled when they shot him, when they drowned him, when they quartered him with horses," Thomas tells me, as we huddle in the schoolyard before the first bell. When it rings, I stay close to him, careful to step only upon stone and clumps of grass. "Each time they buried him, he rose from his grave. They never could kill him."

Thomas is my best friend. He keeps salt along his windowsill to stop Mister Fish from plucking him from his bed at midnight.

There are other children in Mister Fish's belly. I see them in my dreams. They huddle close around Gracie Ash. Like too much fat in a sausage casing, their bare arms up against his skin, threatening to burst their captor. But they won't split that skin. Nothing can.

Charlie tells me Mister Fish is slight. That he leans forward on narrow legs. That his cheeks are sunken and hollow. He must be lying. Mister Fish is a bloated tick in my dreams, stomach distended and hanging with his caught children.

We saw him yesterday. Thomas and I. On the way back from school. It was raining, the sky pressing down on us. I was trying to watch my step, to keep from the lower places filled with muck. Thomas kept pulling at my arm, impatient to get out of the wet.

I felt Thomas' grip on my arm tighten to stone, first, and then I saw those boots of his, muddy and worn. Thomas ran. I heard his footsteps clatter on the uneven paving stones until they were gone and there was nothing but the soft purr of rain. Slowly, I lifted my gaze.

Charlie was right. Mister Fish is a thin man. His lean frame holds no evidence of the children he has gobbled up. He has tight skin, like over-boiled pork. His spine is twisted and it bent him towards me, his milky eyes close and at the level of my own. A white mustache streaked through with grease hung over his top lip. He smelled of tallow and cinnamon.

He started to speak, and I could see the teeth that had chewed up Gracie.

"Happy is he that taketh thy little ones," Mister Fish said in a low, dry voice, "and dasheth their heads against the stones."

I ran, then, my feet splashing against the wet street. I could not see the ground, or the houses, or the people I passed. All I could see was Mister Fish's ribs, like prison bars, with Gracie Ash's face pressed against them, her wide eyes nearly eclipsed by the reaching hands of the other children trapped in that bleak, damp place.

Momma made me wash the floor. When I could not tell her why I was crying, she passed me a rag and a bucket and told me to clear the floor of my muddy tracks. My arms ache now. My own belly is empty, rumbling, and yet I could not find the strength to eat my supper. Even when Charlie threatened to eat my plate himself, I could not bear to lift any food to my lips.

Grey Mister Fish will come for me tonight. I have lined salt on the windowsill, but it will do little to keep him out, to stop him from hooking his thin fingers under the sash. His body will angle into my bedroom from his broken waist, and he will pluck me from my slumber. I know he will, I have dreamed it too many times to be anything but premonition.

In his hut at the edge of town, where spiders crawl between loose stones and floss webbing between the dusty beams, he will sit me next to the fire. I will not cry. I will not run, though he will not bind me. I will stay sitting close enough to the hearth for fire to lick sweat down the hollow of my spine. My eyes will meet Mister Fish's eyes, until those white orbs become my own, until I see what they see.

I will take the meat offered by those dirty fingers and eat of it. I will take communion. I will become communion. I will join Gracie, and we will live forever.

#

Christina Harrington is a writer/editor based in the Hudson River Valley where she lives with her boyfriend, their dog, Rocket, and too many comic books. You can find more of her work in *The Boiler Journal*, OSU's *The Journal, Roanoke Review, Coffin Bell* and others.

Our Dream Town

by Laila Amado

Her body is mangled, broken, dragged through the woods, and dumped on my doorstep. At least, that's what it looks like.

There is nothing I can do, and if I'm careful, if I avoid looking at the bloody heap on the doormat slowly oozing a puddle of brownish gunk, I might be able to hold myself together and not end up sick like the last time it happened, when she was upset and angry with me for days.

I turn and go into the kitchen, take the plates from the dish rack one by one, sort them according to color in the cupboards. Going through the simple mechanical motions helps me stay grounded, stills my frantically beating heart, stifles the rising panic that one day she won't be able to mend herself.

I try not to look, but my eyes seem to have developed a will of their own and my gaze keeps drifting to the thing on the threshold—a bundle of bones and dirty rags dragged halfway through the door.

I take a tin jar with coffee beans from the shelf, throw a handful in the grinder, watch the machine whir. Out of the corner of my eye, I see the bloody pile on the floor shift and rearrange itself.

I set the copper cezve on the stove, the one with a long wooden handle cracked along the middle, the one my mother brought with her, when she crossed the ocean. Mother's voice, matter-of-fact and measured, recites in my head, "Take two teaspoons of coffee, one per each cup, add some boiling water," and a hand shoots out from the bloodied rags, splays five pale fingers on the floor. One is bent backwards, and it trembles like the unfurling beanstalk in a slow-motion video clip.

Foam rises, and the smell of coffee fills the kitchen. I yank the cezve off the burner before it runs over. The pile draped across the threshold extends, shifts upwards with a moaning sound, contours of a body—a shoulder, a hip—visible through the rags. It unfolds upright, sways, makes a few tentative steps.

I'm pouring coffee into the cheerful painted mugs we bought at the summer fair, when she steps through the door and hugs me from behind. She smells of grass, and morning dew, and upturned earth, but the smell of blood lingers in my nostrils.

*

Two days later, her blouse billows up in the bathtub, quivering like a cupola of a jellyfish. I pull clumps of her hair from the drain and they stick to my fingers like seaweed, covered in slime and rot. I'm dry heaving over the kitchen sink, when she comes down the stairs dressed in a fluffy bathrobe. For the rest of the morning, we pretend that nothing has happened.

*

Next time, it's by fire. On a bright summer morning, a cloud of soot erupts in my face when I open the oven door, a tray of fresh blueberry scones in my hands. The smell of burning fat is overwhelming. With my eyes shut, I hear her bones cracking open in the heat.

I'm on my third cup of coffee by the time she joins me, and

I'm jittery and it's just too much to handle, and I beg her to stop.

She looks at me, indignant. "I thought you loved the view from the park by the river."

"I do."

"And the little coffee shop on Main Street."

I nod.

"And the brass band concerts and the very helpful librarian at the new cultural center."

I know where this is going, and I sigh. "We both love this town."

"Yes, and I serve an important function for its people. Every one of them. The monster needs to die for them to feel safe, and so I do."

She picks up her handbag and steps out into the gathering dusk. Outside, the wind chases clouds across the sky. I sit by the bedroom window until the horizon grows light against the jagged outline of trees in the park and the milkman's wagon rattles while taking a sharp turn at the end of the lane. When the front door creaks, I go down into the kitchen and set the cezve on the stove.

#

Laila Amado writes in her second language, lives in her fourth country, and cooks decent paella. Her stories have appeared in *Daily Science Fiction, Rejection Letters, Porcupine Literary,* and other publications. Follow her on Twitter at @onbonbon7.

There Was a Curse Upon Them

by Benjamin Woodard

Against the stream, the air thin and frigid: it is here that the loup-garou pins the man. Gone is the man's wagon, his horse. Moonlight illuminates these two figures and the long shadows of wilderness. The beast's bony limbs shuffle against the man's body. Pelt musk drowns his nostrils.

"Demon, spare me," the man pleads. He shuts his eyes and begins to pray.

But there is no blood, no tearing of limbs. The loup-garou liberates the man, and when he opens his eyes, he spots the short blade normally tucked in his left boot between the beast's pointed teeth. The loup-garou spits the blade to the ground. Streaks of moon kiss the animal's chest, and, crouching now, it gestures a paw at a small piece of parchment tied with cord around its neck. The man takes the slick blade in his right hand. He rises and bends close. He sees that the parchment is littered with letters, but the man cannot read, a disadvantage that brings him shame.

The man squeezes the blade's hilt. His lungs shudder.

Meanwhile, the loup-garou waits, sure the message on the parchment is clear—*Pleas free me of curs cut paw wit nife Save my sol*. The animal gazes into the man's eyes, looking for a hint of compliance. The man waves the blade. He points at the parchment around the beast's neck. Yes, the loup-garou thinks, this man knows what he must do.

The creature extends one paw for cutting.

Yet the scared, illiterate man has merely pretended to read the parchment, out here in the middle of nowhere, the running water to his back. He notes the beast's sharp nails and, rather than acknowledge the passive nature of the loup-garou's actions, feeds off the panic coursing through his limbs. He first plunges the blade into the animal's outstretched paw before slashing its arm, belly, neck, and finally sinking the weapon into the loup-garou's heart.

The creature howls into the dim canopy; the parchment flutters to the ground, and the man runs. He sprints the thick forest until he finds his horse and wagon nearly a quarter mile away.

He tosses the short blade into the night.

He wipes his hands on his pant legs.

He thanks God for helping him flee this nightmare.

And soon, he will tell you and your mother of his bravery, while deep in the forest, the loup-garou will return to its human form and die there against the stream. It will remain in this resting spot until tomorrow, when a foraging teen will discover the corpse of a well-respected farmer. Locals will blame the farmer's death on the creature, though the man, after learning of the body's location, of the cut marks, will know better.

In response, he will drink more. He will yell for no apparent reason. He will break five plates. This fugue will last for exactly three weeks until, one night, awoken from incessant nightmares, he will march into your room and demand you teach him to read. You will comply, but he will continue to drink. He will continue to yell. Eventually, he will open the front door to an abandoned home.

You and your mother will have escaped.

The man will take your lessons in hand, return to the forest, and comb the earth. He will search for the severed parchment, and when he recovers it from layers of leaves and mud, he will parse out each word until he weeps.

You will never see him again.

This is all yet to come.

Presently, though, the man sits in his wagon, thanking God. He pictures your face, warmly lit by the evening fire, a tug of sleep lowering your eyelids as you wait for Papa's return from a long day of labor. A feeling of calm washes over him as he conjures a tale of valor to tell you and your mother. An owl hoots above him. He shakes the reins.

The horse lets out a sigh; it trots a bit faster as it escorts the man home.

#

Benjamin Woodard is editor in chief at *Atlas and Alice Literary Magazine*. His recent fiction has appeared in *Pithead Chapel, Cutleaf, Necessary Fiction,* and *F(r)iction,* and his microfiction can be found in the 2019 and 2021 editions of *Best Microfiction.*

Find him at benjaminjwoodard.com or @woodardwriter.

It Wasn't a Black Dog, It Was Never a Black Dog

by Anika Carpenter

Hedgehogs are noisy eaters. Janet had two in her garden. She named them Horace and Mable after the children she never had. Sat on the iron bench in her favourite spot, under a lampshade moon, Janet thought she heard their usual scuffling and crunching. But it was October, the noises weren't made by hedgehogs. Unknowingly, Janet smiled, let herself be comforted by the rustling sounds, and to be warmed by the blanket wrapped around her. Her favourite, the one that Alan had bought her as a fiftieth-anniversary present. Knitted from mohair, the same brown-grey as a hedgehog's fur. She pulled it tight smiling at the thought of the two spiky creatures filling their bellies.

'Hello my beauties,' she said gently. 'You hunting slugs for me, Mable, you good girl.' She wasn't prepared for a response, for the sound of a familiar rasping tongue.

'You silly cow. Talking as much shit as ever.' The lavender bush shook. Branches of the rosemary snapped like old bones. The voice drew nearer. 'Missed me?' Janet knew better than to scream. Her neighbour's idea of help was very different from hers.

Before she saw him, she smelled him; old chip fat and cigar smoke. A smell that reminded her she could be hollowed out, and filled with crawling, itching thoughts. What had come for her was not a man but a sparrow the size of a man, of a conviction. Its eyes were watery and almost crusted shut. Its beak looked leathery. Earwigs and wolf spiders crawled in and out of greasy feathers and it dragged itself along, not with claws but a pair of hands, child's hands gleaming white-pink in the moonlight. Delicate and clean as the mohair blanket.

Every cell in Janet's body turned pale and brittle. She fumbled for the words Alan would have whispered to her, 'Keep the authority in your voice, girl, that's all you need do.' She tried, she always tried, even when her throat felt as though she'd been forced to swallow unswept leaves, again. 'Get out, you're not welcome here.' The bird laughed, a mean back-of-the-throat laugh that only a person expert at ridiculing a child's proudest efforts could make. 'Silly bitch, I'm going nowhere.' Hand over smooth hand, it moved closer, reaching out pretty fingers with nails sharp as whittling knives. Piss trickled down Janet's thighs and soaked into her pyjamas. The crisp autumn air bit into her arms and everything benevolent was snatched from her.

The sparrow fingered a corner of soft wool. 'Look at this ol' rag! This your comfort blanket, crone?' It wasn't the blanket that was comforting it was the scents sheltering in the fibres; last year's bonfires and Alan's cologne. "Please," she managed, "leave me alone, for once." The bird shuddered disdainfully drew its head into its body and coughed a faecal sack up into one of its tiny hands. Then, with arse-smacking triumph, it slapped it down onto the blanket and crushed it into the soft wool, obliterating all trace of the past. As it admired its handy work, it clenched and unclenched its fist, the way her first husband did when he was trying to keep his patience with her. Janet turned her face as inconspicuously as she could towards the house, toward the door she'd pulled tightly shut to keep in precious heat.

'You won't make it, not on your corn-ridden feet. Even if you did, you couldn't get it open in time. Why don't you ever fix anything? Oiling hinges, not fucking brain surgery, is it Janet?' When the bird spoke something wet and pink foamed at the corner of its mouth and fell in glistening lumps like raw, chewed flesh. Janet's own flesh felt heavy, mawkish as bread dough worked hard and easily sullied. Sudden pain in her right ankle confirmed the bird had a hold of her. It cocked its head at the unswept paving slabs, the rusting bench, the pool of piss at Janet's feet. 'How about you stay out here with me tonight. The air will be vicious cold. Freezing to death would be better than all this, no? Wouldn't it be nice for the neighbours to get shot of you and your nighttime ramblings?. They might have someone move in who can actually look after the garden. Someone who doesn't sit out at midnight babbling on at hedgehogs. Imagine that Janet, someone with a little decorum.'

Janet looked around at the flowerbeds littered with fallen leaves, the clematis vines tumbling over the arms of the bench, roses not yet deadheaded, soil spilling from upturned plant pots. It all smelled so good. This, she reminded herself, was a place for singing and feasting. She straightened up, snatched back her blanket and threw it over the bird, the way you might throw a tea towel over the cage of a budgerigar singing too loudly, too late in the day.

'I will not have you stay here!' Janet yelled as the bird screeched and clawed at her with fingers that were turning grey and forming scales. Using what strength she had, with both arms, she squeezed and pushed down on the bundled creature like someone trying to get all of the air out of a camping mattress. The more the bird struggled, the harder Janet squeezed, and as she did it shrunk. When it got small enough to pass for an everyday garden visitor, Janet brought her fists down on it, over and over and over again, until it was still and bloody.

The rusty hinges sighed contentedly when Janet went back into the house. The hallway's wooden floorboards creaked, 'yep, yep, yep,' as she walked towards the bathroom where she'd run a bath scented with wood chips and Acqua di Parma in which she would soak herself and her blanket.

#

What Happened to John

by Najla Brown

I saw it fuckin' peel John like a grape, but no one will believe me. It took one long, scythe-like claw and separated skin from flesh so fast I thought I'd imagined it.

Then John hit the ground. All capillaries and no face.

Have you ever heard a freshly skinned body slap against the pavement? It sounds like the shit they slop on your tray going through a cafeteria line, but the thing wasn't done yet.

It slipped into John's skin like a hospital gown, tying his hair together to keep the halves closed. It took everything off his back. His shirt, his pants, his fucking *back*, before dragging his body into an alley and walking out wearing John's face.

I didn't stick around to see where it went after that. The next thing I know, I'm coming to in my bed wearing piss-stained jeans, stem still in hand.

That was the last time I saw John's face until it popped up again on the news. Apparently, he had a family. They filed a missing person's report, and the cops are asking for any information related to his disappearance.

But I'm not telling those pigs anything. It's not like they're going to believe me. Hell, I don't even believe me. I was high when I saw it, and I've been real slow to touch the shit since.

I've been going to NA meetings to help me through most of it. It relaxes me to be around other people. I keep hoping maybe I'll see John again. That's how we met in the first place. I guess we both kind of fell off the wagon, but seeing him would prove that I hallucinated the whole thing, and I really need that right now.

I keep having dreams of that fucking thing coming for me, reaching out with those blood-stained razor blades, darkness peering out from behind the fleshy eye holes that used to be John's face. Each night it gets closer like tunnel vision closing in until it's all I see. When it got close enough for me to count the spots John missed when he shaved that morning, I started taking Adderall to keep me up at night.

I'm almost positive all this shit is in my head, but I can't talk to anyone about what happened without getting dragged away in a strait jacket. Besides, the Adderall is helping. I almost feel like my old self again. I even went out to the bar with a couple of buddies. We got a little sloppy, and I ended up leaving with the bartender.

I don't know if it was the sex or the booze, but I slept like a baby that night. I guess she thought I did pretty alright too because she told me to stop by the bar anytime. I decided to take her up on that. It was nice to have a place to go that wasn't a fucking NA meeting.

I started off swinging by a couple nights a week. I've been sleeping fine since meeting her. No nightmares, just dreams about splaying her out across the bar. I told her about those dreams. She said she'd let me do it too, but she'd have to be fucked up.

I knew what she meant.

I haven't been in touch with my guy for a while, but he

didn't ask any questions when I went to pick up the stuff. I didn't see any harm in testing the shit out before I met up with Sherry at the bar, so I ducked into a public bathroom to have a taste.

The Adderall was one thing, but god, did I miss this. I couldn't even remember why I stayed away so long until I stepped out of the stall and saw fucking John's face.

#

Najla Brown is a West Texas native who now calls Houston home. She spends her days writing taglines and her nights writing everything else. Her words can be found in *The New York Times, Redivider, The Coffin Bell Journal,* and elsewhere.

Inheritance

by Jo Withers

On the night my mother died, she laid an egg.

My sister and I were with her at home, just as we'd promised. She was terrified of hospitals, the wards upon wards of diseased last breaths clogging the air like chloroform.

Neither of us had been on the front line with death before, but we knew the end was close. She was weak as a bird, less than forty kilos. When she started thrashing on the bed, we thought it was normal, that death throes were violent and passionate. Her skeletal frame, which had barely twitched in weeks, was jerking and panting like a soul possessed, skin red with heat, limbs flailing at her sides, face strained in effort. As her aching body arched for one last time and her final breath escaped in a swollen scream, a bloody shape appeared beneath her on the bed.

While my sister kissed her forehead, closed her eyes and laid her arms across her chest, I fetched a towel. She helped me roll the bloody thing along mother's thigh into the cloth, watched as I wiped red clots away to reveal the egg, big as an emu's, speckled purple on grey. Neither of us spoke as I wrapped the fragile package in the towel and hid it in a chest beneath the bed. When the coroner came to collect the body, all we could think about was the foreign object in the chest, we couldn't wait to be alone with it and it seemed like an eternity before he'd done the paperwork and trundled mother's unresisting body out of the door.

On the first night, we slept with it between us, one hand on each side. We marveled at its opaque smoothness, and as it grew warmer in our nest of body heat, we kissed it softly and talked to it as though it were a child.

The egg was precious, we must protect it at all costs and so we made a pact, we would never leave the egg alone, one of us would guard it always.

I could work from home, so took the day shifts. The first time I was alone with it, I just kept it on my lap and thought of her. I stroked its surface, trying to recapture those initial feelings of warmth and comfort but it lay there hard and cold against my leg. The more I held it on my lap, the more I thought of death, and it was a relief when my sister came home and took the egg away.

That night, I woke around midnight to hear voices from my sister's room, whispering and laughing. I crept out of bed and silently slid my sister's door open just enough to see inside. She was kneeling on her bed, holding the egg close to her chest and talking to it softly. With every gentle word, the egg glowed red beneath her hands and she laughed as it grew brighter as she spoke.

I returned to my room but couldn't sleep. When my sister came next morning to give the egg to me, it was speckled grey again. As she passed it over, I felt a surge of warmth before it sat cold and hard within my hands.

That day, I spent hours on my bed, stroking it and talking to it as I'd seen my sister do, but it was unresponsive and lifeless as a rock.

Every night and day that followed was the same. My sister would take the egg to her room at night and I'd hear them together, singing and giggling, and knew the egg was glowing bright beneath her hands. Every day, I gave everything to coax a little warmth from the callous orb, telling it my deepest secrets, revealing my most fragile hopes, but the egg sat between my fingers stone-heavy with indifference.

I began to hate the thing. Instead of holding it, I stowed it in a drawer, lonely and ignored.

Then one evening, my sister had to go away on business and reluctantly placed the egg in my care overnight. As she left, she made me promise to keep it close. She'd noticed changes in the shell, it felt hotter, its membrane thinner, and once she was sure she'd felt movement.

I lied and said I'd felt the changes too, that I had seen shapes, spiraling below the shell, that every day I felt its power grow. She smiled and said it was our mother's love. I nodded, clutching the egg to my chest as I waved goodbye, then ran upstairs and threw it back into the drawer.

In the first light of morning, I woke abruptly to a rattling noise and knew it was the egg. As I opened the drawer, it was rocking savagely and cracks were appearing on its surface. As I watched, fragile wings appeared at the openings and a black eye pressed against the shell, dense and penetrating like a crow's. I scooped the egg into my hands and instantly it glowed green and the brittle wings grew larger. I dropped the egg onto the floor in fear and spite and the dark wings began to beat hard, pulling the creature out into the world.

The thing had no resemblance to a bird. It was hideous, skeletal yet hairy, like some prehistoric moth. It buzzed violently then turned and locked its heavy, blinkered eyes on mine. Suddenly, aggressively, it darted forward aiming straight towards my head and I stumbled backwards and lay screaming on the floor as its wings beat fast around my temples for so long and so loud that I didn't hear my sister come home and run into the room.

She stood, framed in dawn's sepia light, gently beckoning it towards her. As it danced gracefully into her arms, she thrust it through the open window into the cloudless sky. We watched as it got smaller and smaller until eventually, only emptiness remained.

#

Jo Withers writes short fiction for adults and children. Previous work has featured in *The Caterpillar, Ghost Parachute, Fractured Lit, No Contact,* and *Milk Candy Review* among other places. Her work was also chosen for inclusion in Best Microfictions 2020 and *Wigleaf* Top 50 2021.

Naught but Shadows Walking

by Levi Krain

Rob was the first to go, although he came back later. The rising sun had turned the lake into a bright mirror of the blue autumn sky when we realized he was no longer on the trail behind us. We searched, of course, the others looking uphill into the woods, calling his name in ever harsher, frustrated bellows with no response.

After a while, I stared out into that lake gazing coldly back. Not a ripple stirred its surface and its secrets remained unfathomable.

"He's screwing with us," said Jeremy.

"Yeah," Steve agreed, then shouted into the tree-filled void, "See you at camp, asshole!"

Later came and Rob was suddenly there, pitching his tent alongside ours. Steve's anger had evaporated and he and Jeremy poked fun at Rob in friendly ways but made no mention of his disappearance.

I grabbed Rob's shoulder. "Where'd you go?"

He turned with dark eyes, like deep pools, but smiled. "Had to take a leak." He turned away and the others ignored our exchange.

Around the campfire, Jeremy and Steve joked and laughed in their usual, drunken fashions. Rob, though, sat a bit further back, only staring at the rest of us with a sloppy smile screwed on his face.

In the morning, I sipped coffee and watched Steve and Rob pack their tents and gear. Steve was grumpy but jocular, his sleep too little and poor but not enough to dampen his large personality. He pointed at Rob's paunch and laughed that married life had made him soft and fat.

Neither mentioned Jeremy, who did not appear and whose tent did not stir. We packed, Steve ate an energy bar, while Rob declined food or coffee and just stood around grinning.

The three of us left Jeremy's tent sitting empty and forlorn like a deserted snail shell, and hiked onward. Steve led the way, as he had every day, and I let Rob get ahead of me, so I could observe him. He seemed taller and fatter, ungainly and sluggish. He walked in staggering, jerky motions and his arms was puffy, swollen, and shiny. The flesh jiggled like jaundiced pond scum.

The day and the trail unfolded sluggishly, everyone subdued and silent except for Steve who talked weather and baseball and lost youth. We camped again in the evening and Steve, maybe sensing the end of the journey or maybe just feeling lonely, spoke loudly and angrily about dead careers, dead friends, and dead dreams before drinking himself into a stupor.

In the morning, Steve's tent did not stir.

I was up and nearly finished with my coffee when Rob squeezed his bulk out of his own tent and unfolded his frame to stand nearly seven feet tall. He was truly fat now, bloated, and his skin rubbery in the pale light.

I poured my remaining coffee on the ashes of the campfire and stood facing him. I frowned. "Why didn't they notice how different you came back?"

Rob gave me that stupid grin, matched it with a stupid shrug. "People don't usually notice," he said with a slight burble. "Maybe they don't want to notice."

"It's a power, or something like that?"

Again with a shrug that sent his whole body heaving like beach surf. "It doesn't work on everyone, though." His eyes were green now, emerald pools above squishy, yellow-gray slug lips.

"Well, it doesn't work on me." Rob's stupid smile slipped as I stepped boldly toward him, drawing a skinning knife from my belt. "Didn't you notice they never joked with me? Never spoke my name? Barely paid me any notice?"

I jabbed the blade somewhere low in his gut and ripped upwards with a strong, swift motion before jumping back.

His mouth and eyes gaped like a dead fish's and his belly opened like a split bladder. Out poured gallons of algae-laced water, lake weed, crayfish, minnows, frogs, and muck. As the Rob-flesh fell away, out slipped the two waterlogged corpses of Steve and Jeremy to flop on the ground.

The puddle of lake water flowed away in a widening circle, only gradually draining into the dirt and sand of the campsite. When nothing moved for a long time, I stepped forward, knelt down, and cut strips of flesh away from all three bodies. With a pang of gnawing hunger gurgling inside me, I began stuffing pieces into my too-wide mouth, tearing flesh and organs with my too-sharp teeth, while my too-long tongue writhed like a sandpaper snake.

#

Levi Krain rose from a clear, cold northern lake and enveloped a small midwestern city. Since then, he has moved on to greater things and now resides in witch-haunted New England where he spins tales and refuses to drink the water from the well. His fiction has appeared on *The Molotov Cocktail, Back Patio Press,* and *Aphotic Realm.*

The Farmhand

by Gareth Durasow

Dad's up to his armpit in a cow's fistula when I tell him what Hector's been saying at school, what he's been calling me since I told him about the farmhand.

He rinses his arm under the standpipe. 'You weren't supposed to tell anyone,' he grumbles, and goes to feed the pigs.

After supper, I'm blowing the yolks out of goose eggs when my phone spasms on the table: COME TO THE BARN.

And then: BRING YOUR PHONE.

I put on Dad's cap lamp. Its clumsy light leads me down the yard, past the burn barrels and heaps of horseshit, and takes me to the doors I've had nightmares about since I was old enough to dream.

The boar is tethered to a pole in the ground. He's so old his forehead has buried his eyes. He breathes like a blocked bathtub. Dad said not to name them, but this one has HECTOR painted across his side in thick red capitals. He says, 'I want you to film it,' and unbars the doors to let out the dark, where the farmhand unfolds like a Swiss army knife.

It screams in the key of flank-gorged spears, and I know well enough to wait until the noises have stopped before looking. Even so, I look too soon. It's wearing the empty pig like a feedbag.

Dad asks, 'Did you get all that?'

I scrub the footage back. Time skips like a scratched vinyl and the pig is restored, frame by frame, sliver by sliver.

'Yes,' I manage, and swallow a soup spoon's-worth of hot sick.

'Send it to the little bastard, and then fetch the wheelbarrow.'

*

Whenever I can't get back to sleep, I write in my dream diary.

I was using a cotton swab to clean the wings of an injured bat when the noise started. It was like our old internet—a robot's impression of a seashell in your ear. I asked Dad, 'Can you hear that?'

'It's the pigs,' he said. 'They're frightened.'

I followed the noise to the barn and stepped inside, onto acres of mirror.

Silence, like I'd interrupted something.

The pigs were lying on their sides, but the strange floor created the illusion of them having been balanced in mid-air—and with it, the threat that the spell could break, and smash them like ornaments.

I recognised Hector, one I shouldn't have named, and ran to him on the footfalls of my upside-down twin. I ran until I had to jog and jogged until I had to take off my boots and carry them.

When I was stood over him, that's when I realised the mirror's appalling trick of the eye, and the boots fell from my hand onto their reflection with a grotesque *slap*. After that, I stumbled from one far-flung carcass to the next, trying to figure out which was the rest of Hector.

Now, like a good insomniac, I wait for my turn to fall asleep again. I listen to the near silence: the pendulum knocking like a hanged man in a wardrobe; the nautical clatter of things swimming through the pipes. It tells me all I need to know; Dad isn't back from the barn.

*

When the door opens, he looks like he spent the night under a horse. I talk through my yawn: 'You should've asked me to help you.'

He's feeling his way along the chimney breast, the spines of his books.

'What's wrong, Dad?'

He's at the fish tank, lifting the lid. He delves inside and gropes around the algal bloom. The fish panic as clumsy hands scramble after them, trawling hell for leather through the gravel. By the time he's finished, the water is a squall of dirt and scales, and every one of them is on the carpet jack-knifing for breath.

'How much have you had to drink?'

It speaks in the voice of wrong radio frequencies—'You weren't supposed to tell anyone'—and with both hands parts Dad's face, like a body bag, to show me what took residence in the place he used to spit and swear from.

I take the stairs three at a time, and the farmhand follows at the pace of sand through one's fingers: a man-shaped eclipse at the end of the hall. Every doorknob betrays me, hemming me into the corner where it daubs on my flesh the only letters it knows how to write, in the only colour it knows to write in.

The first one is H.

#

Gareth Durasow grew up in Castleford, England. His short stories and poetry have been published by *Dead Ink*, *Neon*, *The Rialto*, *STORGY*, *Shearsman*, and *Ad Hoc Fiction*. Find him on Twitter @GarethDurasow.

Climate Change

by Jan Kaneen

That's what they call it, prattlers as reckon there's science in nature, but there's other things shifting than just the weather. Seen it with these very eyes, I have, out in the wilds of the Lincolnshire fens.

Fear or something like it was making me drive too fast that night. I've never been a skittish woman, fen-tiger through-and-through that's me, but I'd been feeling weird since the downpour started—sort of stretched and jangled as my imagination made monsters of the storm. I bucketed the truck round another hairpin bend stopping only inches shy of yet another road-closed sign. Flash flooding's nowt new in the fens these days, but this felt different, like every detour was steering me deeper in.

Waves of rain churned in the headlights swilling names of childhood monsters into my mind—Black Shuck, Will-o-the-Wakes, Ginny Greenteeth—local terrors said to stalk the lonely roads on nights like these. I checked my phone that'd packed up past Crowland but there was still no signal, so I switched on the radio to settle my nerves, but the distorted crackle only echoed the thrash of rain on the thin window, a white-noise thrash that caught the rhythm of the wipers. Tiddymun, they seemed to breathe, Tiddymun, Tiddymun. I shivered as something long-forgotten resurfaced—my Gramma standing behind the bar of the Ferryboat Inn—crossing herself whenever the fenmen spoke that name. *When watter teems these fens agin,* they'd tell travellers, in the old way of tattling, *beware the Tiddymun wi-out a name—grey heer, grey heed, an' walkin' lame, no bigger than a three-year-old bairn. Tiddymun the throat-slitter, Tiddymun the skin-flayer, Tiddymun the scourge o' strangers as show no respect.*

'You're fenland bred,' I told myself out loud, 'from punt to plough. You've nowt to fear in this place,' and as I said it, my gaze landed on an unmarked track hanging pale above the flooded fields. The decision made itself. I spun the wheel and sheered leftward.

On a clear day you can see forever in the fens—no trees or hills to break the horizon, just mile-after-mile of reclaimed farmland, once wild marshes now forced into man-made furrows that sit below sea level, separated by drains that channel the water, and above, a sky so wide it seems to come from inside your head. Not that night. That night there was no moon or stars, no distant windows casting occasional squares of light. The scattered smallholdings that once sat below the road were long-gone, gobbled up by greedy agricultural conglomerates rich enough to keep the waters at bay. That night I almost fancied I could feel the fens seething their need to revert to nature.

The figure flickered from nowhere. I floored the brakes and felt the impact.

Then blackness.

When I came to, a pale youth was peering through the open door, reed-thin, wearing sodden white cotton that seemed to shine its own light.

'The road's a river over beyond,' he said, dripping a finger into the dark, and as I looked, a sudden gust blew a hole in the cloud—a weak new-moon showing a bank of jagged blackthorn, and in the place his finger should have been, the glint of steel. My head swum into darkness again and the next thing I knew he was holding me easy as you might a child, stooping to place me on a small wicker chair in an earthen room that smelt of yesterday. I was weak and addled, with pain stabbing up my legs. I watched silent as he sat cross-legged on the floor opposite, took up some wood and started to whittle—slow smooth strokes—with the knife he'd carried out on the fen, a thin skinning knife with an old-bone handle.

'Speak your name,' he snapped, whittling steady, fixing me with eyes that lit the room.

I shivered speechless for I was cold as winter and couldn't think beyond the rhythmic bite of that blade as it whittled and peeled and peeled and pared. He nodded toward a grey cloak lying threadbare on the dusty floor. I watched transfixed, hardly breathing as it twitched into life and rose above me, but when it settled over my head and shoulders the pain eased and I felt dry and right.

'Think it back,' he drawled, still whittling steady, 'to the fens afore they was drained—to mires and mists and folks as eked out a living, and not a one of them as didn't carry a witch's bottle to ward off the evil.' A crack of shadow curled his lips into a crooked smile, 'But there's no such protections now.' Then he set the wood aside and rose to his feet and as he stood he seemed to grow, or me to shrink, for he towered above me now. The knife flickered like white fire as he drew it back behind his shoulder then launched it forward into my face. Another hair's-breadth and it would have spiked my eye, but I didn't flinch, I didn't blink. I faced into that gaunt steel and watched as it stopped dead. It hung in mid-air. Frozen. Held by nothing. I stared into that pin-prick tip and it seemed so familiar. My hand reached forward and as I took the bony handle, it all came flooding back…roaring back…raging back.

'Speak your name,' cried the Will-o-the-Wakes dropping to his knees before me now, offering up the rough-worked crutch he'd whittled fit for a three-year-old bairn. I hobbled lame to my old-new feet and in a voice that cracked like reeds in a howling wind, I seethed my ancient name.

So call it "climate change" if it makes you feel better, you prattlers as think you know truth from Tuesdays, but this earth's had a gutful of human truth, and there's darker things rising than just the water—darker things than you can ever imagine.

#

The strange and always short fiction that Jan Kaneen writes from her riverside cottage in the vast washes of the Cambridgeshire fens has been published all over the shop, from *Bath Flash* to *Strands Literary*, from *Aesthetica* to the *Fish Anthology*. Her debut memoir-in-flash, however, *The Naming of Bones*, is published only by Retreat West Books.

Ice Window

by Jonathan Duckworth

Every night, the mirror in the hallway of your parents' cabin turns into a window. Every night since discovering this, you've waited for your parents to fall asleep to talk to your friend.

You've been here in the mountains three weeks now, far away from everyone you know. Your friend helps with the loneliness. He's shorter than you, which is one reason you like him so much. It's good to be taller than someone. You wonder if his face is really his face, or if it's just a mask, but you've never asked—that would be rude. Last summer while walking in the woods back home you found a deer's skull; his face looks just like it. He has antlers; big, branching antlers. His eyes are just empty holes. The first time you met, he scared you. Those black holes staring out from the woods, those flat teeth chattering as he shivered. But then you decided to call him Tony—because you always wanted a friend named Tony—and then he wasn't scary anymore. He listens to you when you talk; none of your friends back home listen like Tony listens.

Tonight, you sneak out and report to the mirror. The mirror doesn't show you in your pajamas, doesn't show the hallway or the stuffed goose mounted above your head. Instead it shows you the woods, shows you the skinny, white trees and the moonlit snow falling around them. Where you should be, Tony is standing.

Last time, Tony showed you his new raccoon pet. It was pretty cute, but it didn't move at all. Maybe it was just scared, maybe it didn't like how Tony was holding it by the tail. This time it's your turn to show him something. In your hands you have the newest Spider-Man comic, or at least the last one you were able to get before your parents took you to the Rockies. You don't want to assume, but you're pretty sure Tony's never heard of Spider-Man, so this should all be new to him.

But something's different about Tony tonight. He's much closer to the mirror's edge than he should be. Usually he hunkers back like one of the shy kids at school—another reason you like him—but tonight Tony is close to you, so close the long end of his face is almost touching the mirror. Little circles of fog spread and shrink on the mirror near his nostrils.

"What's up, Tony?" you whisper, "Is something wrong?"

Tony points at you with his clawed finger and then moves his hand like he wants you to come closer. This is new and exciting. You felt bad for thinking it, but honestly, Tony was starting to get boring. You shuffle toward the mirror. Tony gestures for you to come closer again. You can feel the cold coming off the mirror on the tip of your nose.

"Tony, I can't get any—" you reach forward, and your hand touches the mirror, for one instant feeling the cold glass, and then your hand falls through like if the mirror's not there, and hard fingers close around your wrist and drag you forward.

One second, you're tumbling, and the next everything's very cold. You're not in the hallway anymore, you're in the woods. Your feet are sinking into snow, your socks getting damp. The wind blows and you've never been as cold as you are now. Up ahead you see something. Between two trees is a window, floating in the air. You see Tony through the window. He's standing where you were standing. You call out to him for help, but you can't even hear yourself over the wind. There's something different about Tony—he's gotten taller. A lot taller. His antlers are almost as high as the stuffed goose, almost scraping the ceiling. You see his body for the first time, a body of bare bones and pieces of loose skin that hang like the bark on birch trees back home. Tony turns back to you, and you think you see something like a face—something like your face—looking out from a dark hollow place inside of his ribcage, but then he turns away. He's standing outside your parents' bedroom door.

You try to yell again, but the wind takes your voice away. You reach for the window, but your hands only touch a pane of ice so cold it makes the snow and wind seem warm. Through the window you see Tony's wooly, clawed hand fumbling with the knob to your parents' door. Tony turns the knob, and the ice window becomes a mirror again.

#

Jonathan Louis Duckworth is a completely normal, entirely human person with the right number of heads and everything. He received his MFA from Florida International University. His speculative fiction work appears in *Pseudopod, Beneath Ceaseless Skies, Southwest Review, Tales to Terrify, Flash Fiction Online,* and elsewhere. He is a PhD student at University of North Texas and an active HWA member.

FRENZY

**"If there is to be art...
one physiological condition is
indispensable..."**

– Friedrich Nietzsche

Sleeper

by Stephen Hundley

There's a bomb in the water. Dropped by mistake. One plane touched wings to another, and in the fire and snapping metal, in the crash that scattered birds and made ticker-tape of the marsh grass and carved a long and muddy row, the bomb was lost. Eaten by the waves and now sitting in their belly.

Covered by sand leached from the wide ocean, blanketed by silt snaked from rivers and fields and, somewhere, the feet of mountains, world weary, at last dissolving and giving themselves to the processes of time, come to cup and hold and press the bomb that lies swaddled and gurgling atomic equations to itself, perhaps looking up through Saint Catherines Sound and seeing the suggestions of stars on an enormous mobile. Perhaps feeling kinship with the celestials. Knowing that it too will burn itself to quick splendor and hot death.

Infant Star, the bombers named you Mark 15, but you've been cut from them and left to something wilder, where bottlenose dolphins puzzle at your devil dagger fins and big ocean-liner rays gust over your head.

A Mustang broke its face against a tree, and the tree kept growing, folded itself over the steel. The acorns grew to saplings in the folds of the backseat. So like the barnacles gilding your sides, little bomb, stacking one on another, little beaked mouths opening and loosing seed: you're a bloom.

Come a hurricane and a past life while the waves lift and throw you. For a second, flying in the ocean dark, you are at 30,000 feet and counting the seconds until the lever is pulled and you scream, nose first, for the concrete. Hurricane Dennis, like a child's clumsy hand, makes sputter Spitfire noises with its lips while it lifts and drops you, makes you fly.

If bombs have blood, yours has run hot from the tumbling, end over end, across the sand floor until you rest, lodge again, at the foot of an island with its beach stripped and drawn out long and shallow beneath the water so that the sun can reach the bottom where you rest, letting daylight touch you and the mirror moon trace your bulge beneath the sand. The sun is touching you, and you are touching it back, glimmering sweet.

Some think you're sleeping, but you're a bomb, dreamless and awake. You've been faking all along, while the undersides of turtles loom black above you and men jet around. What have you been thinking of all this time, if not of your arrival to the halls of short and violent fission. You must be aching inside that shell. In the half light of summer, with the sun so long in the sky, so even the fish grow bored of treading water, you must be drunk for change. You must be smitten with combustion.

The water runs warm here. The grey sand like a skirt in high wind. Hiding and flashing steel. You must be singing, thinking: I'm in love.

I'm in love, and nobody knows it but me.

#

Stephen Hundley is a former high school science teacher from Savannah, Georgia. His work has appeared or is forthcoming in *Prairie Schooner, Cutbank, Carve,* and other journals. He serves as the fiction editor for *The Swamp* and is a Richard Ford Fellow at the University of Mississippi.

For the Birds

by Amanda Crum

I am not your version of Death.

Slatted teeth, a dirty skull hidden beneath blackened folds. A scythe, sharpened to an edge and ready to cut down the wicked. Be honest; you've seen that version in your mind's eye, yes? Perhaps even feared it, dreamed of it, doodled it in the margins?

That's not me. I'm more bone than flesh, it's true, but there are no tools fashioned that are more effective than my own hands; a cloak would only slow me down. Where my shoulder blades should be, there sprouts a pair of golden wings so magnificent they might make you weep if you could feast your gaze upon them (you can't).

And why should you require wings? you might ask me (if you could). It is not to hover over a farmer as he works his field, or to make an easy job of taking the moribund woman who lives in a New York City high-rise. My wings carry me across the tumbling oceans, over ruined desert landscapes, from oak tree to bonsai. I ride the thermals behind birds and insects. Those are my target.

You might rail against the thought that such beautiful creatures require their own Master of Death, or the idea that they should deserve their fates. You are not alone. Many have wept at the sight of a fallen robin lying stiff in the grass, at the sound of hungry babies crying out from the nest. Humans rarely have an affinity for death, even when it brings only release.

It is not about what the winged ones *deserve,* but rather what they *deplete.* When they have used all the resources they are allotted, it is my job to call time.

What happens next? you might ask, but I have no answers. That is not my job.

*

Lately, I've been thinking that I might have a time limit, just as the birds do.

I've never entertained the notion that I should want something else, never thought that perhaps there lives a being above me whose only job is to wait. I have been content to watch, to follow the cycle of the Sun and Moon as they meet the horizon, but now I have questions circling in my brain. I realize that contentment has only fostered a false sense of security.

I have never met another Master of Death. We don't mix. It's better for everyone that way, but it makes for one hell of a lonely existence; I can't be seen until it's time. Imagine, for a moment, how it might feel to know that no creature alive has ever looked upon your face. To exist in a state of in-between until you are necessary.

The worst part is that I have no one to guide me, no words of comfort but those I make for myself.

*

I'm good at what I do.

I crouch low, hidden well in a maple tree. The cardinal never sees me coming; his is a good death, a quick one. When he falls like a whim of poppies, I follow to the ground and study him for a moment. I wonder, not for the first time, what might have been behind those intelligent eyes when the future came for him.

When the air changes, I pull up, folding my wings with a hush. Above my head and in the distance, a murmuration of starlings has formed. They seem to hover, then change direction in that eerie way they have.

I watch for a long moment, time drawing out like warm taffy. They are here for me; I can feel it like a feather drawn across my back. Their shadows move like oil slicks across the deepening sky, pushing the air before them with a rush. Soon I can hear them, a chorus of wings and hungry voices rising in a frenzy as they descend upon me.

And I think, *here are the answers.*

#

Amanda Crum is a writer and artist whose work has been published in *SmokeLong Quarterly, Barren Magazine, Lunch Ticket,* and more. In 2021, she was the recipient of the Diana Woods Memorial Award for Creative Nonfiction. Amanda lives in Kentucky with her husband and two children.

Penetration

by Alpheus Williams

Once I dove nights, skimming along sandy bottoms and sharp coral reefs. Ocean predators love night, they feel vibrations, panic and distress, read them like neon signs along a fast-food strip mall on a highway to the netherworld. They smell fear, injuries and blood, so it's best not to bleed or panic. I watched things burrow, shelter beneath the sand, under reef ledges, in small caves. I watched silent predators cruise like shadows suspended in a liquid sky. There is a haunting stillness to it. Water surges over shallow reefs and shatters into glittered silver. There's beauty in the exhaled ascent of your bubbles to the corrugated ocean surface where the moon shimmers like fear.

Once, I ventured into the darkness of an underwater cave. Swim-throughs, where you can see the opening on the other side, framed by rough, rocky walls of darkness. I calmed myself and rode a sweeping current through that dark tunnel. I became trapped at the exit, my tank tintinnabulating on the roof of the cave like a giant monastic bell, my shoulders bumping into the sides. I could see freedom but couldn't touch it. There was no going back. Swimming against current with a tank strapped to my back and lead weights was not an option. I didn't favour crawling along the dark bottom, upsetting carpet sharks, wobbegongs, and other critters with sharp teeth and no tolerance for intruders. A conundrum. I could remove my tank, my link to life and breath, shove it through the hole, follow after it. A calm, calculated manoeuvre, but I wasn't calm. I turned over. Supine, my face towards the blackness of the cave roof, I grabbed the lip and worked my way through. I never entered a swim-through again.

Once, I dove to dark colourless depths into the hull of a wreck, a penetration dive. A large, looming hulk mortally wounded by torpedo in the Pacific War. A great gaping hole yawned in its metal side. At forty metres, sunlight struggles to exist. Our bottom time was short. Three or four minutes, no more. Algae like fine dust collected undisturbed for decades, it coated the surface of sake bottles and human skulls that burst into powdery dust when touched. I took a compass reading. There were three others. I didn't know them well. It was a charter. We swam through the ragged wound into the dark interior. A careless fin kick released a shower storm of silt. Watery dust fell in a blinding clouds. Surrounded in inky darkness, the dim light of the entrance was lost.

I swallowed panic. Inhaled. Pressed the compass to the glass of my mask. Five measured kicks, a dim corona of light. Two kicks. Freedom. I heard frantic clangs of bodies slamming into the iron walls searching for light.

I ascended to a line of tanks, the first decompression stop. Grabbed a regulator, breathed. Heart pounding, ecstatic in escape, guilty in surviving, struggling for control. I looked down at the wreck, checked my watch, eight minutes waiting on the line like a baited hook before I finned to the next stop. A cloud of grey burst through the hole in the ship, a diver emerged. Hope. A halo of light hair. Her name was Iris. She finned towards me. Then something else. A lean, human shape, half again as long as her, webbed, taloned, and scaled. Eyes solid black larger than jam lids. Eyes for dark places. Fast and liquid, it was on her, an explosion of dark blood, limbs tumbled to depth. It came at me, gaping mouth in primate head. I dropped my weights, filled my vest and kicked, rocketed to the surface.

They said I shot through the water like a balloon, delirious, hysterical, incoherent, screaming in pain. They hauled me aboard writhing in agony, vomiting, scratching at my skin, drawing blood. I was restrained, sedated, and flown in an unpressurised plane to a decompression chamber.

Nitrogen narcosis and air embolisms are not conducive to a lucid mind; my account was dismissed. A rescue party, professionals, returned with body parts. Their consensus was sharks driven to frenzy by divers' panic and first blood had made a picnic of it.

*

I love the sea, but I no longer dive. I feel safer on the surface, around people. In the evenings, my minder wheels me down to the promenade. I can watch the lights of the city, the huge clown face of the amusement park across the harbour, the tranquil flow of ferries on the water, traffic crossing the bridge. When I watch these things, it makes it easier to believe I never saw the thing I think I did.

#

Alpheus Williams lives and writes in a tiny village tucked away along the coast of NSW, Australia. He spends a lot of time trying to explore and understand the unseen beauty of things.

The Eternity Ring

by Jan Kaneen

I jolt awake. What broke my dream? A scream in the passageway outside the scullery? A strange compulsion draws me downstairs and a vague feeling it was thus before.

I creep by candlelight down five flights, tiptoeing into midnight's kitchen, but there is naught to see beyond that dark window save my own wide-eyed reflection. I smile, amused by my foolish fancy, and sit myself down at the servant's table, gathering my wits and wishing for daybreak. No more drudgery for me tomorrow. That is what the master said.

"No more," he spat, his pale cheeks yet tinged with passion. "I know what I must do." Then he took up the brass-handled poker and jabbed at the embers in the dirty hearth as if his irritation might rekindle them to flame. "Go now to your bedchamber, and at first light, away on some small errand to the bakery or butcher, that I might tell your mistress with you gone from the house."

At daybreak, I don the moonstone ring he gave me leave to wear indoors. What need for secrets now? My belly will tell all, soon enough. Striding out from the servant's hall, I am sure as Sundays it will be for the last time. I stride across the courtyard over the uneven cobbles and swing open the wrought-iron gate. It moves heavy and silent as I pass through into the redbrick passage beyond, then out into the Crescent. I meet no one as I go. The town is grey and dull and empty of everything save clags of mist hanging heavy over the dirty river. It reminds me of childhood, that lazy river, drab and slow and dark and dangerous. I cross the hump of the old stone bridge, and my father's face slinks into my mind's eye. You durst not touch me now old man, I tell it.

I walk down South Brink and round the corner to Barton Road, where Molly Clingo's bakery is quiet and shuttered and there is no smell of fresh-baked loaves. But I am not surprised. I half-knew it would be so. It is the urge to return that takes my breath away, a passion that I cannot resist, so I hurry back as fast as I can, brimful of excitement for my brave new future. I move through the passageway shadows once more, stopping a moment before the gate. I count to three inside my head before raising my hand to push it open, looking through the curlicue swirls of hammered metal, at the pale mist hanging grey over the greyer cobbles, but it swings itself forward with ne'er a touch from me, creaking and cawing like the call of a crow, and as it does, the mist before it swirls and thickens. I watch transfixed from the safety of the shadows, not breathing, not moving, caught fast in the moment, because something is stirring out of that thickening mist, a thing strangely familiar like a childhood scent or half-remembered dream—the wraith of a girl becoming clearer as she moves, and following behind, something darker.

A raised arm, the glint of brass, a sickening thud as metal meets skull. A savage blow—enough to murder—but not enough to stem the frenzy. More blows rage down again and again, smashing, staving, cracking, splintering. I flinch and wince at every stroke screwing my wide-eyed terror tight shut. But the sound is just as fearsome as the seeing, breathless grunts, the sickening thrash, the fracturing cracks that go on forever. Until, at last, a sort of slackening. Deeper breaths and slower strokes—dull-wet thuds that conjure a brutal reality.

I force my eyes open and step forward and the words seem to scream themselves, "For pity's sake, just stop."

The shadow spins round to face me square in a ray of impossible light—my master, his arm raised to strike once more, his pale cheeks spattered red with death. He tilts his head, first this way then that, staring through me, seeing me not. My gaze sinks to the broken creature twitching at his feet, the crimson-grey mess where its head should be, a flailing hand lying palm-down perfect on the gory cobbles, and on its finger, catching the last of the fading light, the milk-blue ghost of my moonstone ring. In that instant, before darkness falls, I see everything, understand everything.

I jolt awake. What broke my dream? A scream in the passageway outside the scullery? A strange compulsion draws me downstairs, and a vague feeling it was thus before.

#

The strange and always short fiction that Jan Kaneen writes from her riverside cottage in the vast washes of the Cambridgeshire fens has been published all over the shop, from *Bath Flash* to *Strands Literary*, from *Aesthetica* to the *Fish Anthology*. Her debut memoir-in-flash, however, *The Naming of Bones*, is published only by Retreat West Books.

In the Darkness, There Is Light

by Paul de Denus

No hurry, the mission did not expect him back until Friday. Plenty of time to be careful, to do it right, just as he had done all the times before. No need to be careless now. Yet, something told him to hurry. The exchange of the monies had gone smoothly, without incident between him and the men from the mountain, the ones dangerous and unpredictable. But that would end soon; he had acquired more than enough money to leave all this behind for good. All that remained was to dispose of the body.

He stopped his digging, quickly lit a favored cigarillo, the kind he got at the little shop in Carrizal. He exhaled the fragrant smoke into the morning air, watched it trail and vanish along the horizon where a black mesa sat, a rising coffin against the changing stained-glass sky. Soon he too would vanish, disappear from this wretched country to begin a new life, the life he deserved. He scanned the deep blue terrain around him. Here his congregation slept. There were no markers but he remembered all of them, all the ones he had buried.

"Eternal rest," he murmured. "Better for them this way. Better for everyone."

He had gladly taken the monies they had entrusted to him, money to give to the coyotes from the mountain, the men who would take them across the border. But God's will had always been the better plan. "Better off to be with Him in His kingdom than to struggle in the earthly life they would only regret." The man inhaled deeply from his cigarillo. The demise of these lost ones was a blessing, a good deed perhaps. He did not see it as murder. God knew of and understood these things.

The man adjusted his collar and resumed the dig, the spade crunching through the loosened dirt and rock. The grave was shallow, a mere scratch along the desert surface. He laid the coat-wrapped body in the shallow groove in the earth. It lay barely below the ground. "This one, truly an abomination—but all here are God's creatures." He looked about, a thin quiver vibrated across his puffy lips and he smiled. "Soon, little one, soon the creatures from the earth will come for you. There will be peace." With his toe, the man nudged at the body, knocking and tucking small rock next to it, absently kicking the small jar that rolled from inside her coat into the brush, the lid dislodging. A centipede raced out, climbed the man's shoe, a firefly lit on his pant leg.

The woman watched her daughter kneeling in the dirt, the child's hands busy in the halo of light from the leaning lamppost. The girl was observing something, a centipede, those of many legs, wriggling over her withered hand. The black bristled hairs on the girl's arms stood firm, quivered. The woman watched as her daughter gently dropped the centipede into the small glass jar, its movements quickly disturbing a nest of beetles, worms, and spiders. The girl looked up into the ink black sky, her bulging eyes dark as oil. Like lightning, she flashed a spindled arm in the air. She brought her hand close to her face, partially opened her wilted palm revealing the luminescent green glow. A firefly. "Look mama!" she uttered, her voice in a guttural tone, as if muzzled. "Light, to show the way." The girl hurried the firefly into the jar, struggled to place the punctured lid on top. The mother scanned the dark, crooked street, touched her daughter's misshapen shoulders and gently guided her into the house. Put the jar in your coat, Magdalena. The priest will be here soon.

In the early light of dawn, desert predators were at work. Rattlesnake and viper, their numbers uncountable, wove their way through the lavender and short grasses. A mass of tarantula spread for miles across the desert floor, parading over a trillion fire ants in a wide swath, the hiss and click, a slow wave moving. Spider and scorpion, beetle and lizard danced over each other, the grotesque caravan advancing. Jack hare ran. Fat beaded Gila monsters, eyes black as death, skittered across the ledges, dropped to the rocks, their angled mouths grinning in an open cry. The desert floor tumbled and spilled and roiled with urgency, the surface rippling like a heat haze. They clambered toward the luminescent green glow, eyes on the dark silhouette framed against the dark blue horizon.

The desert moved, a soft swell all around him, and he thought it was the shimmering grasses swaying in the wind, but there was no breeze.

#

Paul de Denus publishes excerpts from the novels he's never written. That was one of them. He lives in Richmond, Virginia.

Underbelly

by Alice Kaltman

A gushing fountain of silty, soiled water spews like a geyser from the kitchen sink drain and spills to the floor. Every inch of turquoise tile is now a liquid landmine. I slosh around in leaky rain boots, holding my phone, and curse the day ten years ago when we moved into this place. Ten years of repeated mistakes—mostly mine—which hounded us like relentless arctic winds. My husband and I chilblained explorers without the proper gear.

Now, I am alone in this dribbling disaster. My husband has left this junk heap, fixer upper, false-promising house. He fled six months ago from the rotted ceiling joists, the toxic mold under the children's bathroom sink, the nail-popping, wide-beamed floors. And, of course, the septic tank out back that should've been replaced eons ago and is now announcing itself in an effluvia mix of human shit and rancid piss.

But in truth, what he escaped: emptied amber glass vials I buried deep in the geranium pots, the emergency gallon of Tito's stashed behind the extra toilet paper in the pantry, the tiny plastic bags that refused to flush down the toilet, rebels floating to the surface after I'd left them for drowned, greeting him when he went to pee, fly unzipped, lid open.

My husband took the children. No blame there.

Take me away from here, I pleaded twelve years ago in the hazy beginning when the fact that I always had a third or fourth drink hadn't bothered him, when we both thought change was possible, when we didn't know the me who raised her spittle-smudged glass was like a scabby apple fallen from a diseased tree with a thud, doomed to rot before I even hit the ground.

The busted septic continues to pulse out dirty secrets. Sludge is rising. It smears the legs of the kitchen table. The tiles covered in cloudy murk, are now the sickly ash of asphyxiation. I sit on a chair with my knees to my chest, an array of poisons displayed on the gingham cloth much like my mother arranged after-school snacks for me when I was a kid. I'd eat supermarket brand vanilla wafers and withered grapes while she sat across from me with her needy, lovelorn bloodhound eyes and her tumbler of gin.

You like it, baby? she asked, her slurred speech a garbled hornet's nest. Your favorites, right?

I'd nod and chew, nod and chew, shove cookie after cookie between my lips, a thick paste of cheap cream lining the roof of my mouth, grape skins wedged between my teeth, until my mother laid her head on the tablecloth to moan and, eventually, to snore. I'd stare at the specks of dandruff and line of skunk-like grey hair along her part, waiting for the cursed snack-stone in my belly to turn into churning slop, at which point I'd rush to the bathroom and hurl.

Now I think how the optimism that comes with a starter home and starter babies only lasts so long when you're the kind of woman who, like her mother before her, prefers to hide deep in her own stinky burrow, hoarding shortcomings and sins like dirty tissues wadded up to block the entrance.

I choose each poison carefully. I drink. I smoke. I snort. No more off-brand cookies for this girl. I watch the rising miasmic tide from my perch. Seepage from my own dark underbelly. I toss my rubber boots in and watch them float like jaunty little barges towards the living room. I chuck my phone into the sewage and watch it gurgle and sink. I could save it, I could call someone, but I hold off. Everything will be alright, if I can just hold off.

#

Alice Kaltman is the author of the story collection *Staggerwing*, the novels *Wavehouse, The Tantalizing Tale of Grace Minnaugh*, and most recently *Dawg Towne.* Her stories can be read in *Vol.1 Brooklyn, Lost Balloon, The Pinch, Hobart*, and *Joyland* among many other cool places. Alice lives, writes, and surfs in Brooklyn and Montauk, NY.

Only Four Letters Arrived

by Jaylee Alde

My Dear Old Neighbor,

You were like a photograph. The kind people kept in their wallets until nothing but the edges were left. I didn't mean to do it. I hope I didn't scare you. It was just a picture. I am well-intentioned. Sometimes, my hands are not mine and I do things. It's not my fault.

I am a different kind of animal. You know this. I see the true faces of those around us. You do too. How their shadows shake behind them like an angry fist. Their indignation manifests into a coat of mean sap, clogging all the bits of kindness left in their guts, leaving heavy drips of it in grocery aisles and sidewalks for us to slip on.

I see how desperate they are to uncoil and how that desperation rots them from the inside out. It is ugly. They are all ugly. Sometimes that rotten scent they give off invades, it slithers past my defenses. It seeps into me like thick mud and I can't scour it off and I disgust myself because of it. You are not one of them.

Understand? I know you do. Maybe it's because of the way you love light. I've watched you, head bent towards the sky in the dead of afternoon, at your window, eyes closed and in prayer.

Before you, my dear neighbor, I once thought the world was only made for hammers, only built to house the noisemakers, and I was drowning in it. Not anymore, and it's all because of you. In you, I found a calm tide of soft things and a love for light.

I want to tell you about my day. It was not uneventful. This is why I'm writing to you now. I truly believe I saved your life today. I stood in my kitchen eating a fat plum over the sink when I saw it. An apparition, a sneaky thing but with hard edges, like an outline, slithering along the borders of your yard. I know, this sounds crazy. I thought I was going crazy as well, but the ghost hit a beam of light and its true nature revealed itself. A beast with loose skin and covered in black maggots that swayed as one with each step the animal took. Its eyes were human—bloodshot and filled with thirst. Its teeth were bared, snapping at the wind like clapping knives. I sneaked behind the beast as quiet as a forgotten book. Without hesitation, I lifted the thing by its neck—the maggots falling down my arm like the juice of a plum—and I slammed its face into the concrete base of your home. I repeated until the monster went limp. It is now buried under my back porch if ever you require proof of my heroics.

I must go now. I'll see you soon. The sirens are growing louder.

With all my love,

Stuart.

*

My old neighbor,

I will get better. The doctors have said so. I don't like it in here. Everyone's eyes are dead and ugly in here. Not like yours. And why did you say those things about me in court? That wasn't nice. I'm sorry about what happened, but I can honestly say it was no longer the animal you thought it was. It sounds silly, of course, but nonetheless, my accounts of the day were entirely accurate. I can't help but feel you are ungrateful.

You shouldn't be mean to me.

We were never strangers and you know that. But I did enjoy how pretty you looked in court. How stoic you were when the lies about me fell from your mouth like broken teeth.

Honestly, I don't blame you. I don't blame you for this bleached, bone-white room I'm sitting in now. I don't blame you for all these numb days I sit through daydreaming if your sun looks the same as my sun. I don't blame you for the heavy curtains, with thick stitching that reeks of vomit, that I stare at until my eyes bleed. I don't blame you for this cloud of mumbled babble that I endure when all I want is a quiet place away from the loud thud of drums that vibrate off all this fucking ugly. Honestly, I don't. Someone made you tell the court those lies about me. I know it. I'll see you soon.

Love,

Stuart.

*

My neighbor,

They let me out last night. I don't understand why you've never written back.

You should have written me back.

Do I still scare you? Is that it? I shouldn't. I am obviously a harmless bug to you. Obviously, a lost plastic toy. A sad sack. A whining dog left out in the rain. I'm nothing to you, right? Do you still hum a childish song in the kitchen when no one is home? Do you still open all the windows on bright afternoons? Do you still close your eyes and soak in all that light?

Even if I wanted to hurt you, I wouldn't.

Sincerely,

Stuart.

*

You have a beautiful family now.

You know who.

#

Cohabiting

by Trahearne Falvey

Our existence with the bugs was not understood by family members, but it gathered its own logic as the days chugged on. They crawled at night from books and behind pictures, and hid themselves impeccably in the daytime. Though they left marks on the skins of our guests, our guests returned, having left their blood. At times, we could even enjoy the knowledge of crushing them, our bodies so much larger than theirs and heavy with sleep. We considered naming them.

One night, however, a guest arrived who was different from the others. He lay like an elephant seal, wreathed in a fug of grass-smoke, and left cartons of banana milkshake to go sour. Always, we could hear the beeps and crashes of his video game humming through the damp walls. He read Husserl, did not shower, and, just once, was caught for shoplifting flowers. We hosted him because we loved him, or were supposed to, or because he had nowhere else to go.

As the bugs multiplied in the warm veins of our mattresses, our peace unraveled. We began to toss our limbs around deep into the night while the ceilings above us moved. We would wake weak with hunger, white as dawn, then spend hours vacuuming walls. We sent hysterical emails. We scratched all the time. Our sheets, which had been Twombly canvases, smears and splotches on white, became almost Rothkos, saturated and overwhelming, and it was difficult to discern whether the red that pooled and bloomed was our blood or theirs, if there was a difference at all. The red would not wash out, became brown and purple, cooked into the cotton, and when we hung the sheets over the curtain rails to dry, the rooms flooded with a dreadful glow.

There were men who left bombs on our carpet and told us to vacate, but when we returned, nothing had happened. There were men, speaking only through actions, who told us we were going mad.

As they grew fat from the iron in our blood, the bugs' appetite became insatiable. They balanced on the rims of wine glasses and drank the dark liquid, they tore holes from the loaves of bread in cupboards. We found them in the refrigerator among the oranges and milk, swarming around the shrink-wrapping of a pair of pork chops, increasing in number until it seemed as though every surface of the house was only a shining, moving black. Our emails became incoherent, all in capitals, drenched in the details from our fitful, sweaty dreams and terrors. Our skins peeled from the scratching.

One night, we dragged our bodies from our beds to the kitchen and whispered our fears while the video game pulsed its noises from the other room. Had we noticed, we asked, that our guest's books did not send tables scuttling on opening? Or that his skin was spotted only with milk-induced acne? And was it possible to make out an almost perfect circle of clear, light space around him, absorbed in his flickering game? The bugs, we agreed, could not make their home in the creases of the sofa where he slept, and it had made them crazy. If he would only leave, we said. But we loved him, or were supposed to, and, besides, he had nowhere else to leave his body.

Our resentment grew until it filled the flat and cast a shadow over our guest's screen. He paused his game, brought us all into the circle to listen. He would change, was changing: he had taken out the recycling, had washed his hair, had been wired money by his father. It was a good sofa, he said, a place to sleep. When he said the word "sleep," we became aware of a hunger that had sunk into our bones, and we shook together, gathering heat. We could see the bugs beyond the circle twist their heads towards us, perching on the tip of their leaf-shaped bodies and glinting rust-coloured in the light from the television monitor. Too many to name. Some strange intelligence, hovering in the air between antennae. They were interested in our anger, wanted blood that warmed and moved. No, we said, no, and we found the strength between us to push our guest from the circle. They swarmed into his absence, embraced our bodies, and all light went dark.

#

Trahearne Falvey is a writer and teacher based in South London. His stories have appeared in *Mycelia, Algae, Short Fiction,* and *Necessary Fiction,* among others, and his criticism has appeared in *3am Magazine, Entropy,* and *Sabotage Reviews*. He was the winner of the 2020 Aurora Prize for Fiction.

Lovesong

by Alice Maglio

It ended. With a gun. Like in a Western, but in the woods. And no standoff. Just the one guy. So, not much like a Western at all, except, maybe, for the stakes: a child, specifically, a daughter. A pearl of greatest price. A mouthless river. A suggestion of a wing.

This daughter became not a daughter but a gap.

The guy behaved as a person might when forced to contend with a gap, that is, not well. He emptied out his apartment, emergency sidewalk sale, but he didn't stick around for the dollars from the women with lavender hair. He couldn't deal with the extra furrows in their foreheads, with the seeds of the things they'd say later on landlines to their friends and grandsons: the vague image they'd sketch of him standing, lanky, about to be toppled over by the light breeze. The grandsons' inevitable boredom, their restless fingers.

He thought of Prufrock, specifically the lines, *In the room the women come and go / Talking of Michelangelo.*

He couldn't remember any more lines from the poem, but he

did know it was about growing old, and something about a peach.

He let his sideburns run free.

He stopped going to his job. He had some money saved.

He made coffee, now, by boiling water in a pot and pouring it over grounds in a mug, then straining that liquid into another mug through one of 50 filters in a pack from CVS.

He'd met his ex in grad school. He liked how her incisors looked a little fangy. She had a name that was popular in the '90s but now felt a little ridiculous, nostalgia heavy, and no one wants to go back to the '90s and its not quite solidified aesthetic—wannabe millennium babies living in fear of Y2K.

When his daughter was born, he insisted they name her something verging on old fashioned. At least the name would point to times in history filled with innovation and forward movement.

He drank his coffee. He contemplated the fibers of his wall-to-wall carpeting. He had no power to avoid clichés.

It's amazing how long a day is.

He sat in awe of this.

His daughter had gradually stopped talking to him. How does a nine-year-old gradually stop anything? Taper off. Shoot back some methadone.

The prospect of acquiring drugs was too exhausting to consider.

He knew of course that it wasn't the daughter tapering but the ex. Extending the rectangle of her phone less and less in the direction of the girl. And when the ex did extend it, he imaged her keeping one eye trained on the little one, maybe making her face more sealed up at every laugh, more relaxed at every frown, every beat of silence.

The last time he saw his daughter, she squirmed in a restaurant booth. Mostly she looked at her plate, her water glass, the window. She held her mother in her face. She responded politely to his questions but didn't ramble on about whatever she was doing that day, earlier in the week. Her restraint devastated him.

He stared at the woods from his kitchen window every time he made coffee. Was that rustling in the brush a deer?

He could insist on seeing her. He could insist on regular calls.

He counted forward in time, year by year. Each year guaranteeing he'd occupy less and less space where she was concerned. He calculated how far he could stretch.

It was surprisingly easy to purchase a gun.

When his ex was pregnant, he'd lay his head next to her stomach at night, feeling slightly ridiculous, like an expectant father in a movie. He wanted to assure the baby, give her preemptive advice, suggest a plan for how everything would play out. But he didn't want to tell her the wrong thing, so most nights he'd end up falling asleep, silent, the strength of his intention playing against taut skin.

#

Alice Maglio's fiction has appeared in *DIAGRAM, Black Warrior Review, Wigleaf, Pithead Chapel,* and others. Her work has also been included in *Best Microfiction 2020.* She is the book review editor of *The Rupture,* and she holds an MFA from Sarah Lawrence College.

The Spare Room During a Storm

by Meg Mulcahy

The sound of the ghost watching them was deafening over congealed plates and scummy teaspoons.

'We're going to have to do something. A sage, a chant. Something. Get someone in,' she had once insisted.

He nodded silently. They hadn't slept for months, they hadn't touched in just as long; for fear of being watched. Feeding off this fear, the ghost was now reducing them to tears. It must have grown bored with domestic bliss and their pathetic attempts at tolerance. Now was the time to really wreak havoc. The damp, the noises, the creaking of wooden floorboards in the middle of the night. Love was the grime in the skirting boards and the bloody dregs dried at the bottom of a non-wine glass. The ham-handed fingering of delicate curls at the back of her neck despite all her teachings. The mug of tea waiting for him after the shower.

Love was also the hole in the wall that would never be filled. The bathroom that they'd waited two years to paint. The holiday that kept being promised. The cards and texts she'd send his family from both of them because he insisted they 'didn't care about that kind of thing.' The razor that never found its way back to his shelf, making him late for work.

The ghost was done with their performance. Their ineffective rituals. It was going to have a go at reclaiming its home, they decided. It would let out gushing water sounds like a hose being let loose, rusty cranking, a screaming boiler, and pointed knocking on the walls whenever the inhabitants had rationed a moment's peace. It was using their spare room as its own brass band rehearsal space, complete with traumatised audience.

When the pair couldn't take it any longer one particularly terrifying Tuesday night, they scraped up as much strength as they had left, collected it in a dustpan and moulded it into the shape of a couple. A couple that had been each other's emergency contact, confidante, funeral-goer, best friend.

Clammy hands held tight, they walked down the hallway towards the noise with phone torchlights enabled and the tall umbrella for protection. As they approached the bedroom, one last heavy step was enough to crack the sodden board underneath cleanly in two, unleashing a ferocious hiss so violent they jumped back. A host of flashing silverfish erupted from underneath, spewing forth in a fountain so vast it looked as though it came from the Underworld itself—squirming, crumbling insects jumping from all sides as the wave grew higher in liquid rubble. All this time, festering. No ghost, only rotting.

'We can't stay!' he bellowed, eyes wider than she'd ever seen.

'We just can't. We have to get out.'

She gazed agape at the mouth of the silver fountain, numb.

'We have nowhere to go,' she replied quietly.

Panic-stricken, he allowed himself to stare at her in disbelief for a second before rolling up his sleeves and barging past her into the kitchen. He flung open cupboard doors, slamming one off its hinges and dislocating a full drawer of woolen spools, rolled up plastic bags, photos and fridge magnets. Shopping lists and electricity bills flew out of them and surrounded him like a flurry of cherry blossom petals welcoming their time to move on, flooding gutters with desiccated pink coconut.

He rifled through them, his hands feeling for the rounded bottles of health-store supplements he knew to be there. He landed on several rolling jars and quickly scanned the labels for items he knew to be good herbal solutions for treating silverfish; diatomaceous earth, citrus essence, lavender. He racked his brain desperately trying to remember what she'd said all those months ago.

'It's in the pipes, love.' She rubbed his back gently. 'I think it's too late for all that.'

#

Since filming, the Dublin-based poet and piss artist Meg Mulcahy moved into a retirement home for herons. Her work can be found in *Janus Literary*, *Okay Donkey*, and *Kissing Dynamite Poetry*. She was longlisted for the Cambridge Flash Prize 2020, and tweets @TheGoldenMej.

Apocalypse

"…and I feel fine."
– R.E.M.

Angels Only Dance with Astronauts

by Donna L. Greenwood

There are days when it all feels broken. Sometimes, during the period we designate as daytime, I look at my colleagues and their faces elongate like stretched chewing gum, and when I look again, they snap back to normal. Some days, time shatters around me like an old mirror and shards of yesterday and tomorrow slice their way into the present. They're just hallucinations, I'm used to them—we all are. After six months in the space station, they are a daily occurrence for us. The dancing angels are the worst—those streaks of light and dazzling flashes that come out of nowhere. The experts back home tell us not to worry; they tell us that the flashes are caused by cosmic rays, that they are free-moving subatomic particles from distant destructing stars. I'm not convinced.

I'm ready to go home. I'm exhausted all the time. I'm weary of not being able to feel the weight of my bones. We all are. We are the final three, left here to switch off, clean out, and tie up loose ends before we climb into our shuttle and head back to Earth.

Bogdan Yahontov is making his way to the cupola. So is Yui

Tanaka. I make room for them so we can all see the view. We've had the same idea—one final look at the Earth before we leave the space station. We turn in unison and look through the windows at the planet outside. It is breathtaking even after all these months—our beautiful blue planet shining with life in the everlasting black. Bogdan Yahontov puts his hand on his chest and looks at Yui Tanaka in a way that finally explains why, whenever I see them, those two are always together. For a while, we stand there, three different nationalities united by the sight of one beautiful globe. I can't enjoy the moment though; I feel agitated. There is something important that I need to do. I close my eyes and try to remember.

When I open my eyes, Tanaka and Yahontov are gone. I push myself out of the cupola and down the long tube that leads to the communications hub. When I get there, I see both astronauts clinging to one another. Their silver tears swim around their heads like transcendent fish. Yahontov points to the communication panel and shakes his head. I float over to the transmitter and shout panicked questions to mission control but the only answer is static—the line is dead. I move over to Tanaka and touch her arm. She smiles apologetically and then crumbles into dust. Her ashes swirl around me in infinite motion. Heart blasting in my chest, I turn to Yahontov. When I see his face, I scream. His lips are stretching over his head; they split apart and reveal the red, grinning skull beneath. I push myself up and away from him and head back to the cupola.

When I get there, the sight through the windows snatches the breath from my lungs. The Earth is not blue. It is the dark orange of a smouldering fire. A memory untangles itself from the recesses of my brain. I remember. The Earth has been that way for weeks, ever since the fury of those first missile strikes.

There is something I need to do. I manoeuvre myself out of the cupola and move to the kitchen area. The bodies of Yui

Tanaka and Bogdan Yahontov are floating above me. They both overdosed not long after we lost contact with Houston. The oxygen levels in the space station mean that their bodies decompose slowly. The sweet, cloying smell of their rot clings to the air. Each morning since the world died, I remind myself that I must eject my dead colleagues, but then time splits and my thoughts float away like Yui Tanaka's tears.

When the lights appear, their brightness is unbearable, irradiating everything around me. Long white fingers unfurl from the luminescence. They reach for me. Somewhere in the distance, I hear music—an old song from years ago. Images of all the lost things expand and shrink around me, disappearing into the dark singularity of a pin prick until I am the only one. I watch the angels dance to the music of the universe. They beckon me and I step forward, finally joining them for the last and brightest dance.

#

Donna L Greenwood lives in Lancashire, England. She writes flash fiction, short stories and poetry. Her work has been nominated for Best Small Fictions and Best Microfiction. You can find examples of her work in *The Airgonaut, Spelk Fiction, EllipsisZine, The Corona Book of Ghost Stories* and, of course, the one and only *Molotov Cocktail.*

Pets

by Nick Story

When it became clear that their owners were not coming back from wherever they had been taken, I let all the pets out of the building. A few cats, but mostly dogs. I figured they'd have a better chance outside.

"Go forth. Find happiness," I told them. But they just hung around out front. They'd gotten used to it here.

I watch the dogs from my window. I recognize a few of them. The poodle from 3A. The dachshund from the fifth floor. The crazy-eyed beagle from the basement apartment.

They sleep in piles near the hedges, or in the weedy flower bed.

They forage for garbage or rats.

They lope and chase each other. Sometimes I go out and throw the ball. The furry bodies fly full speed up the empty street after it. When it rains, they either sleep in the hallway or stay out and get wet.

They seem to be waiting for something. I wonder if they miss their owners. A nice thought, but it seems unlikely. The world isn't nice like that. And yet they remain, which is surely evidence of something.

I try to remember their owners, but some link has been severed. Dogs are the main event now, not the people who had taken them on walks, forced them into Christmas sweaters, talked to them like they were babies.

There's still plenty of nonperishable food at the grocery stores, because the only human left to feed is me, and I don't eat much. Sometimes I pick up food for the dogs. They all love the tinned sardines. The dachshund is the only one who will eat the canned green beans. This is why she is my favorite.

When I go for a walk, they follow me. We form a pack. They've designated me as their leader, which is a mistake on their part. I've never led anyone anywhere.

I feel as though the dogs expect something of me. Something big. Deliverance, probably. Strangely, I expect deliverance too, though not from myself. Never from myself. And I should say "hope for" rather than "expect." And only on certain days.

I sometimes wonder why the men who relocated everyone did not shoot the pets. I suppose they wanted to conserve bullets. I heard about this in a movie once. I can't remember which movie. Some character talking about the value of every bullet. The movies can teach you things. I wish I could watch one now. The days are long and shapeless.

The wind is loud at night, I've discovered. So are the barking dogs. I follow their conversations when I can't sleep. There is a chat going on all over town. I wonder if they discuss different topics, or if the conversation is always about the same thing.

I suppose my main feeling most days is that I am now an unclaimed person. I used to feel claimed by my girlfriend. My mom. A friend or two. Even by the building itself—this is my stairwell, my mailbox. Now nothing pulls me in any particular direction. I could do anything. I sometimes dance around naked. I sometimes talk to myself in bad English accents. But these stones sink to the bottom of the pond without a ripple. The dogs certainly don't care how weird I get.

The other day, the beagle and the dachshund got in a fight over some dead thing. I ran out to break it up. The beagle bit me on the thumb, drawing blood. I hit it and it ran off, whimpering. The little dachshund from the third floor seemed grateful, looked at me with her ridiculous pointy face.

I went in and washed the cut. I saw myself in the mirror. The dirt, the shaggy beard. Seeing myself like that made me wonder why I was still here, that is: why the men who came—in a hundred semi-trucks to round everyone up—had left me in my apartment.

Maybe they left me so someone would be around to admire their work. After all, if the town was completely empty, if *nobody* was here, how would you know it was empty? You needed at least one person to witness the emptiness. But if someone was here witnessing the empty town—even if that someone was just me—then it wasn't really empty, now was it?

And it wouldn't have been empty anyway, because the dogs would have been here.

I must have left my door open, because when I came out of the bathroom, the poodle, the lab, and the dachshund were sitting on the couch. The beagle was sniffing around in the kitchen. They were making themselves comfortable. As if they belonged.

#

Nick Story is from Columbus, Ohio. His fiction has appeared in *The Indiana Review*, *The Common*, and *Monkeybicycle*.

The Story Collector

by Quentin Norris

The earth was no longer green and blue, but grey and dead. Wastelands spread to the horizon, eaten up by the smoke of a fire that burned away all the green and evaporated all the blue. Only a few remembered the world as it was, and their numbers grew smaller every day. Although the odds were against them, they could never give up. It was in their programming.

One of those remaining few was Storybot 415, which was quite literally on its last leg. It was the duty of a Storybot to travel from town to town, sharing and collecting stories from any humans who would listen or speak to it. But Storybot 415's duties would soon come to an end. A rabid dog had ripped its left leg off in the middle of the night while the bot was recharging. It had gone over the data and deduced that it should be able to make it to the next Pit-Town without its battery dying.

The calculation must have been off, for Storybot 415's right leg gave out just as it could see the Pit-Town's burning gaslights on the horizon. It was night and the grey world was full of black shadows. The only light was the distant Pit-Town, taunting the Storybot with its failure. The Storybot did not feel shame, although it could recall the feeling from the stories carried in its database. It rolled over on its back and stared up at the sky. It knew that at one point in time, there would have been stars staring back down because of the stories. It did not understand beauty, but it understood these little lights in the sky once meant something to the human race.

The Storybot could not feel boredom, but it felt the need to pass time, waiting for its backup brain battery to die out, so it replayed the stories saved inside its head one last time before they fizzled into nothing. Once its backup battery died, just like stars, the stories would twinkle out, never to be heard again. The Storybot could not feel remorse, but it understood the devastation that would come about because of its failure, even if the humans didn't.

The backup battery lasted longer than the bot thought it would and it found itself looking up at the morning sky after going through every story. They were truly lovely stories. Stories of happiness, pain, loss, and gain. The human race was truly a remarkable species when it wanted to be. The Storybot would have liked to have seen the world before, it thought.

After another hour of staring up at the grey sky, the bot heard the sound of scuffling feet. A grubby face appeared in the bot's vision.

The face of a wanderer.

The man's skin was dirty and scarred by the poisonous air. He had patches of hair where his beard hadn't fully fallen out yet. Storybot 415 knew that its end had come. Foragers and wanderers only ever wanted one thing from Storybots. If it was not in such a vulnerable state, it may have been able to defend itself, but in its current predicament, its fate was sealed.

The old wanderer judged the bot with beady eyes hidden behind filth. The wanderer set the bot back upright and leaned it against a rock. The Storybot could finally see the rest of the barren world again, and a clear view of the hunchbacked man crouching in front of it.

"Ya don't look good, friend." The wanderer's voice sounded like he made a habit of swallowing a mixture of bees and marbles. The Storybot shook its head. Its squealing gears caused the wanderer to grimace.

"No. Backup battery will be dead soon." sputtered the bot's voicebox.

"That's a shame. What happens after that?" asked the wanderer.

"Every story saved on my database will be deleted" stated the bot. The wanderer's expression softened.

"Damn shame. So you're one of those Storybots, huh?" To the chagrin of the wanderer, the Storybot nodded its head and its squealing gears echoed across the empty landscape. "How many stories you got up there?" The wanderer flicked the Storybot's weather-rusted skull.

"One thousand two hundred and fifty million."

The wanderer gave a low whistle. "That sure is a lot."

Without another word, the old man set down the sack that the Storybot had wrongly analyzed as a hump and dug through it with spindly fingers. He pulled out a perfectly good Storybot leg, although it was from a separate model. "Picked this bad boy up in a cave a few weeks ago, or maybe it was a few days. I can't remember. Anyway, not sure if it'll work, but lemme give it a shot. Should have a battery in here somewhere too."

The wanderer ducked out of the Storybot's view and tinkered for a few minutes, the sound of whirring was the only things the bot could hear for a bit. The Wanderer poked his head back into view with a big gaping grin on his face.

"Success!" he screamed. The Storybot felt a jolt of power in its legs and found itself able to stand fully upright. It did not feel gratitude but it knew how to express it.

"Thank you."

"No problem, ya big hunk of junk. Get on to wherever you were goin'. Oh hey, before you do, though..."

The wanderer stood on his grimy tiptoes and whispered into the microphone on the side of the bot's head where ears would normally be on a human's. The man told the bot a story and the bot listened and retained it.

It was a good story.

#

Born in New Orleans, Quentin Norris (he/him) has always loved storytelling and has been creating new worlds inside his head since before he can remember. He pursued this passion at the UNCSA School of Filmmaking where he graduated in 2012 and has been writing short fiction and film essays for ten years. He currently resides in Winston-Salem with his girlfriend and six pets.

Warden of the Sun

by Chris Panatier

I walk through the garden carrying a twenty-pound bag of birdseed and set it down in front of the first feeder. A house finch and a late-season nuthatch gobble at the last few seeds until I touch the tube and they bounce to a nearby branch, happy to wait the minute it will take me to recharge the buffet.

A rustle behind me. I turn, expecting to see a cat or a fat squirrel out for an easy meal. It's a little girl. Maybe eight. Mouse brown hair, heavy eyebrows. Blue smock.

"Can I help you?" I ask.

"Not really."

"Alright," I say, pausing. Kids are weird. "Do you live nearby? Have a name?" I fill the feeder.

She glances at a patch of daisies. "Daisy."

"Daisy, huh? Okay." I unhook the next feeder and top it off with seed. A solid week's worth. The girl raises a curious eyebrow. "What?" I ask.

She shrugs and pulls a fistful of safflower seed from the bag, triggering an immediate swarm of big, glossy starlings. They throw themselves at her outstretched hand and peck at the contents until her palm is clean, save a few pinpricks that well with blood.

"Why would you do that?" I ask. "Their beaks are sharp as nails."

"I don't normally get this close," she answers. "I like them. Their heads shine like black rainbows."

I cap the feeder and move to the next. The girl—*Daisy*—follows.

"So," I say, throwing her a glance. "Shouldn't you be with your family or something? They say the front edge of that flare could get here today."

"Coronal mass ejection," she says, correcting my terminology. "It's almost here, actually."

I don't know how to process this. I take a long inhalation through my nose. There's honeysuckle in the air. It's spring.

"Rebirth," she says, as if adding commentary to my unspoken thoughts.

Her manner, the way she speaks. Confident. She seems to welcome the coming catastrophe. "How do you know it's coming today for sure?" I ask. I had hoped that maybe the estimates were off.

"They were," again answering a concern I'd not voiced. "The aurora will be something to see though," she adds brightly, as if it might lift my spirits.

"An aurora in the daytime?"

"It will shine like streamers before it cuts through the magnetosphere," she says. "Before…you know."

A weight of sadness descends as I resume my work. I scoop some seed at a platform feeder but halt before dumping it. "So it's really going to…kill…everyone?"

"One does not sling this much plasma to leave any doubt." She plucks a fuzzy leaf of milkweed and turns it over for me to see. A transparent chrysalis shows an almost fully developed monarch rolled within. Daisy caresses it once with the pad of her finger. "Come on out, little guy." She looks at me. "It's a few days early, but he'll be okay."

The chrysalis begins to vibrate and it breaks. I drop my scoop. "What did you just do?"

"Just giving him a few minutes in the air, Michael."

Coaxed from its hibernation, the butterfly pumps its wings until taut and flutters out over the garden.

Any awe that her prestidigitation garners is short-lived. I feel myself sneering. "Why are you doing this to us?"

"You did it to yourselves."

"What are you talking about?"

She holds her arms wide. "You had all of this."

"So, you're just going to destroy it?"

"You didn't recognize it for what it was."

"I did."

"Well, most didn't. And as a result, I have to start over. Rework the experiment, all that. I stupidly assumed that delivering you into a paradise to evolve and learn would have fostered boundless progress. It did for a short while, but then you stalled out. Ambition begat progress but it also begat greed, which led to resource destruction, subjugation, war. Relentless circular descent. It was my fault. I set your ambition too high and your empathy too low. Next time around, I'll reverse them. It might take longer, but at least then you'll have a chance to make it."

"Who are you?" I can't believe I'm going to say it. "God?"

"Not the moniker I'd use. Presupposes the singular. Every star has a keeper. I'm the Warden of the Sun."

"What did you mean when you said *then we'd have a chance to make it*?"

"Make it to the point where a species advances far enough to identify and commune with its star's warden."

"What then?"

Daisy weaves her fingers and stretches her arms behind her back. "Then we talk."

"About what?"

"The things your brains will be capable of understanding by the time we meet."

The sky begins to brighten, warm yellow-orange like a marigold. The birds still flit from one feeder to the next. I uncap a nyjer feeder for the finches and add seed.

Daisy grunts. "Tell me something," she says. "Why do you continue feeding them?"

"Well," I press down the lid, "they don't know it's the end of the world."

"Hmm," she looks upward. One horizon is hot pink, the other electric green. "Would you like to watch it with me?"

I point to the birds. "I think I'll stay with them."

Daisy pulls up next to me and holds my arm. "Okay."

Colors oscillate above us as ribbons of the Sun's flesh burn through the atmosphere. It is as beautiful as she'd promised. There's heat. A flash blinds me. Eardrums explode. I do not feel my own death.

But then, slowly, my vision returns. The garden and birds remain—we remain, protected within an empyrean dome of her creation. The outside world is a blackened husk. Her lips move, and though my ears register nothing, her voice comes clear in my head, booming and leviathan deep.

"I will begin again with you."

#

Chris lives in Dallas, Texas, with his wife, daughter, and a fluctuating herd of animals resembling dogs (one is almost certainly a goat). He writes short stories and novels, "plays" the drums, and illustrates covers for metal bands and books.

After the Ghosts

by Christopher Stanley

The stairlift stutters as it approaches the top of the rail and I worry I'm not going to make it. My wife waits for me in our bedroom doorway, wearing clothes I don't remember—a light cotton camisole and patterned leggings. She steps forwards, her lips as full as her smile. "Won't you join me?"

Seven months ago, we woke up and the sky was cerise, or lilac, or fuchsia—no one could agree. Trees and shrubs were the white of snowflakes and ageing teeth. Roads were the colour of dried blood. The government urged us to stay indoors until this new phenomenon could be investigated, but we were curious. We searched everywhere for the greens and blues of our youth, but they'd been erased from the landscape as though they never existed.

It wasn't just the landscape that changed, it was us. Everyone woke up with skin the colour of bone. White hair with flecks of blue and gold. Eyes as black as the River Styx. We looked at each other like strangers and wondered if we were ghosts. But we weren't ghosts. Not then.

Jean, my wife, finds me at the dining room table, still in my wheelchair, sipping from a glass of water. I don't know where she goes when she's not around. "Have you run out of food yet?" she asks. I have, but I don't say anything.

We adapted to the new colours, somehow surviving the inevitable travel disruptions and empty shelves in the supermarkets. Scientists hypothesised and tested but were unable to reach any persuasive conclusions. Pit vipers, pythons, and vampire bats have thermoreceptive organs capable of registering infrared light, but we don't. Chemically induced colour blindness seemed more likely, but tests for elevated levels of carbon disulphide and styrene came back negative. Fringe groups argued for a variety of psychological, physiological and environmental causes, but provided little or no evidence to support their claims.

Jean started going to church again, and she wasn't the only one. Science was failing us, so an intervention by some higher power seemed the most plausible explanation.

In whispers, we spoke of Revelations.

Then we saw the ghosts.

They appeared quickly and in vast numbers, as though they'd always been there and we just couldn't see them before. In horror stories, we're taught that ghosts are anomalies—lost and lonely, limping down dimly lit corridors, scraping nails across chalkboard walls, faces twisted in pain, mortal wounds visible for all to see. In reality, they were young and vital—friends and families restored to their prime. They thrived in daylight and danced in the dark. They needed nothing. They wanted nothing. We watched, breathless, as crowded streets were overrun with beautiful, incorporeal spirits.

Jean finds me in the kitchen. Every single cupboard door is open. The worktops are strewn with out-of-date condiments and dried herbs. There's nothing to eat. Nothing to drink. I'm on the floor, hunched over and sobbing. Jean points to a paring knife on the wall-mounted rack. "How about this one?"

After the ghosts, people examined their lives and found their prospects of happiness were lacking. What was the point of carrying on? Here was a chance to say goodbye to ageing and chronic pain, high rents and low-paying jobs, abusive relationships and unrequited love, climate guilt and environmental devastation. For most people, the choice wasn't life or death, it was rat poison, bleach, or sleeping pills? The number of ghosts swelled rapidly and the only ones with regrets were those left behind.

Across the world, industries perished overnight. Infrastructures collapsed. Shortages of food, medicine and hygiene products followed, and no amount of government assurance could persuade us there was enough to go around. People who had already lost loved ones found they were starving and out of work. And the smell! The air became a dark river of excrement and decay, to which only the ghosts were immune. While we fought over perfumed face masks, the souls of our dearly departed crowded the streets in an ever-growing party of youthful exuberance.

I follow Jean into the garden, to the cherry tree where I found her body. "It'll be over soon," she says, her cheekbones as sharp as they were when we first met. "I'll stay with you."

I turn the knife over in my hand, feeling its weight, wondering how it came to this. "Why did you do it?" I ask. "Were you sick? Or was I too much of a burden?"

A gentle breeze tugs Jean's hair into her eyes. The collar of her blouse flaps against her neck. She chooses her words carefully. "I thought it would be easier if I went first."

"Easier?"

"For you. To give up. You were always so stubborn."

I roll up my sleeve, exposing the long, black veins snaking up my arm. Then I press the tip of the blade against my wrist until I've drawn a single bubble of blood.

"What's happening?" asks Jean. She stumbles backwards,

raising her arm to shield her face. Her hair whips wildly as though she's caught in a storm. Except, there isn't any wind. "Help me!"

I reach for Jean's outstretched hand, but something tugs her away from me. I drop the blade and roll after her, determined to not lose her again. She stumbles backwards and I lunge for her, ignoring the pain in my arthritic hips and shoulders. For a second I think I've done it, I've caught her. Then her expression becomes one of horror as my hand passes through her incorporeal form.

I watch, helpless, as she rises like a child's kite, lifted by some ethereal wind. The sky is full of ghosts, thousands of them, screaming and flailing as their bodies are swept upwards, spiraling and swirling ever higher into a sky that's either cerise, or lilac, or fuchsia, with just a hint of blue.

#

Christopher Stanley lives on a hill in England with three sons who share a birthday but aren't triplets. When he's not hiding from cloud gods, he's the author of numerous prize-winning flash fictions, the darkest of which can be found spreading misery and mayhem in his debut collection, *The Lamppost Huggers and Other Wretched Tales* (The Arcanist, June 2020). Follow him @allthosestrings.

Bone Stew

by Samantha Jean Coxall

In this town, the dead outnumber the living. The number's something like a thousand to one. We don't have the normal tourist fodder. No big, stony mountains that look like papier-mâché when backlit by sunset on a postcard, or a ghost mansion where somebody worth something lived or died, or even a decent restaurant for people passing through to eat at. All we have are stretches and stretches of shallow hills in every direction, all pockmarked with sun-bleached cemetery stones.

The ground is full and no one bothered to think about what to do about it until it became a problem. At first, you'd just hear the gravedigger guys swap stories about digging a new grave only to find it already occupied. How it's too much a hassle to find space six feet under for an empty plot. Now they just throw two or three bodies in the same hole. No room for glossy funerary boxes anymore. Making bone stew, they call it.

And everything was fine, for a while at least. Until the spring sky swelled with rain and the floods swept through the hills, and with them Mr. Asimov—who died two weeks previously—came floating through town square like it was a theme park lazy river, minus the inner tube. A record year of rain. No matter how many times we buried them again, the bodies just kept slipping and sliding down from the hills, bumping into houses, getting T-boned on mailboxes. You had to check under your car before you started it, just in case a cache of the departed were caught up behind your front tires.

Then it didn't even take rain to bring them anymore—once they knew the way. They showed up on doorsteps like old relatives. The clatter of bones against pavement at midnight. With nowhere to rest, they try to make their way home again and again.

We're tired of digging and digging and digging. The ceremony of saying goodbye does not get easier each time but instead weighs down our hearts with new knots of scar tissue each time we dress in our mourning gowns.

And so now we make do. We find them jobs. Just little things like holding up yard sale signs on street corners and weighing down lawn furniture on a windy afternoon.

My neighbor owns the secondhand store on Main Street. It's mostly the usual offerings: piles of clothes and stacks of ratty paperbacks and altar-like displays of lost and forgotten family heirlooms. He's started taking loose bones, too. There's so many of them. He says: *Look—no more rocking tables*. And he puts a star-shaped vertebra under a table leg. Marks it $2 with a neon sticker.

He used to sit under the store awning next to a metal rack of that day's discounts with a construction paper sign (*We Got Great Deals!*) propped up between sloping stomach and thigh while he flipped through the newspaper, so close to his face you can see the damp ring of his breath seeping through it.

Now he's got dead bodies—slouched against the window, heads rolled back—dressed in patterned sundresses and palazzo pants. You can see the clothes better that way. *See, look how nice*. He thumbs a sleeve.

There's one across the street from me, propping up an

umbrella on a bench with a dozen bus schedules in the front pocket of his collared shirt. I can see him from my bedroom window at night. The milky white glow of him so vibrant, I can't help but wonder how he's not alive.

I watch him each night before bed, waiting for movement in those bones, my own vibrating under my skin. As if calling out to a long-lost friend.

#

Samantha Jean Coxall is a writer and illustrator from the forests of Colorado. She writes about cryptids, ghosts, and grief. She currently lives in Tucson and shares a life with her deaf French Bulldog.

Dead Trees Give No Shelter

by Dom Wilton

It's late afternoon. In the bedroom, the paint is peeling off the walls. It used to be white, pure white. Now, it's turned a sickly yellow, falling in flakes like ash to the bare floorboards. It seems as though the house is decaying, shedding everything which made it a home until just the skeleton remains. Timber beams are visible where the paint is thinnest, like bones in a necrotic limb. This house, it is just a roof and four walls after all. Everything else comes and goes. Tastes change. That vase which was in vogue last year seems so painfully hideous the next. A new face enters and tears down the wallpaper of the previous widowed occupant. The bed where she died is sold for something more fitting to the young couple. The old study, long unused, becomes the nursery for their child soon to be born. Even then, that sky blue room will evolve. Posters on the walls, clothes across the floor, candles, incense, girlfriends, boyfriends. Embalming keeps the form of a person, but does nothing for the substance. Everything that ends becomes new. That's what we believe.

It's comforting to think that someone will find use in what we leave behind. We show each other our favourite things just to see that same spark mirrored in another set of eyes. There wasn't any blossom last spring. That was my favourite time of year. I don't remember when the last blossom was. The ground outside was thick with a putrid mulch. I remember the smell. I remember the rain. It rained for weeks, maybe months. I've never seen rain like it. The few leaves that remained on the trees previously helped shelter the house, but they were gone. It was deafening. Then, one day, silence. I opened the door and stepped into the yard. You could barely call it rain. The water just hung there, gossamer-fine like time had stopped. There was no birdsong.

Under the windows I hung small boxes filled with fuchsias. They're my only real addition to the place. I remember helping my mom plant them in the garden when I was small. I used to love the way they'd fall and cascade pinks and purples over the white fence. She said they reminded her of dancers. I still think of them that way, adding motion and texture to this old, plain house. That's what life is. Anything less is just existing. Anything more is a luxury. On summer evenings I would sit in the yard until the blue sky was replaced by stars. There's nothing in the world to make you feel so small and insignificant than being outside civilization and looking up at the stars. Our happiness, our suffering, our perfect little homes mean so very little when you put it into context. It's amazing we do anything at all.

I never had children. It would have been cruel. I don't think I have much affection to give to others. That's why I chose to come out here. I'm quite happy being alone. I may lack affection, but I don't lack empathy. All that talk of not wanting to bring children into a world with such a sense of impending doom seemed so cynical and hysterical. It's just a protracted suicide. We can't know the future for certain. Surely, it's better to keep going, making positive changes, and hope for the best. We're a pretty resilient species. For all their advocacy, I don't think these people have really spent time out here. If they had, I'm sure they would think differently. Unless they are all like I am in lacking certain capacities, I find it hard to stomach the thought that someone could be so callous and self-important to deny future generations the chance to see what I see now. Even in this decaying state, it is still beautiful.

It's painful looking out through the yellowing nets to see a world which should be so green. I don't know if this is the same everywhere, but I can't help feeling that it is. The last time I saw another person was some years ago, before all this. They hadn't got lost, these two, they were just driving around, exploring. I liked that. They seemed friendly enough. The driver was a young woman about 23, definitely not older than 26. I assume she was just out of college. The passenger, a man of about similar age, it turned out was her fiancé. I asked them if they needed help, but they said they were fine. They just wanted to stretch their legs. They asked me about my home, how long I was living there, why I moved. It was nice to talk to someone. They seemed like they really were interested rather than just being startled by my presence. The way their hands searched for each other, wrapping fingers through fingers. It was love, pure and innocent. They must've stayed walking for a couple of hours. I said goodbye when I left them to do my laundry. When I came back, their car was gone. Only the tracks of their tyres remained in the soft dirt road. After a week of wind and rain, those too went.

*

It's twilight now. It comes around quicker than you think this time of year. The shadows are long. It's not just the house that seems skeletal anymore. My silhouette is rakish, like that of an unwelcome spectre in an old horror movie. The tree branches lattice the ground. They will for many more years until a strong wind comes or the rot sets in. I wonder if there'll still be termites or woodworm. I saw a bird the other day out the corner of my eye. It was a fleeting glimpse, but I'm sure it was real. I'd hate for it just to be bugs that are left.

#

The Favor

by Bill Richter

Five days ago, Aaron asked me to kill him. I'd never killed anybody or ever considered it for a second; I am ultimately a meek person. But I was Aaron's only friend left and the only person he could trust. He was my only friend, too, so I understood his asking me. I told him I had to think about it, that it was an enormous responsibility and I was also concerned about how it might screw me up. We were all pretty scarred from living in a post-apocalyptic world as it is.

We'd had fifteen days warning that the mountain-sized asteroid, what we've usually referred to as "that big fucking rock," was going to hit. The question was where the impact would be and whether it would be on land or in the ocean. I was living in Los Angeles and left immediately. After Covid-19, I was prepared and had a plan for whatever the next event would be. I'd inherited a cabin in the mountains from my parents that I didn't tell anybody about. I packed and headed there after the first news report. There were three other cabins in the area and their owners arrived soon after. We agreed to help and protect each other when necessary, and to give each other space most of the time otherwise. We maintained a regular Sunday get-together to check in with each other, share resources, and make sure everyone knew what day it was.

After the asteroid slammed into Nebraska, the first months were rough, but we had generators that helped us weather the worst of it and guns to fight off the crazies who came through. Food, winter clothing, sleeping bags, and masks were our most important possessions.

I didn't know Aaron before. He knew Herb and Kathy, my nearest neighbors. He stayed with them occasionally, and we'd end up talking. He'd been an architect in Los Angeles and I'd been an animator for movies and TV, doing a lot of work creating cityscapes. Besides talking about post-apocalyptic living, which everyone did, we talked about buildings, architecture and eventually reading, which is what I spent a lot of time doing. I was reading long books I'd claimed to not have enough time for before. At the time I was reading *War and Peace* and I've already finished *Don Quixote, Infinite Jest,* and *Moby-Dick.*

When he wasn't here, he had a place near Los Angeles and he'd tell me about how things were there.

"It's still pretty scary," he said one of those first times we talked. "People are settling down and it isn't as dangerous, but it's still really unpredictable. People freak out and most of those people have guns. Any group that has more than a few people starts feeling like a cult really fast."

That was also my experience any time I ventured out for supplies, or to get a change of scenery for a couple of days. All groups of any size have a leader, and the leaders have something about them that just isn't right. I stay away from most people.

"Why do you keep going back?" I asked.

He shook his head.

"What?" I asked.

"It's going to sound insane."

"Look at our world. How crazy can it be?"

That's when Aaron told me he was vampire, and could prove it.

"I go back because there are people there, and they have what I need."

"Blood?"

"Or the means to get it," he replied. "I don't need it as often as you've seen in movies or read about, but I get sick if I go too long without it. We still don't usually need to kill people to get it. We have other ways."

"You're serious, aren't you? This is real?"

"I was turned six months before everything happened. Eternity sounded much better then."

He left for a moment and returned with a kit filled with transfusion supplies and an ancient medallion.

I believed him, and he told me Herb and Kathy knew too.

A few months later, Herb and Kathy ventured out for supplies, which usually meant clothes, blankets and canned food, and never came back. They said they were going to a different place than usual, always a risk. I didn't suspect Aaron had anything to do with it even when he showed up right when they said they'd be back. He spent a lot of time looking for them and I went out searching with him. He was genuinely troubled by their disappearance. Other than one trip back to Los Angeles, he started living at their cabin.

Then five days ago, two years into this, the thought of eternal life became unbearable for him and he asked me to kill him. I didn't want to.

"Can't you kill yourself?"

"We can't. I've tried fourteen times. But others can, and you're my only friend. Please."

Knowing how bleak my future was and that his was worse, I

reluctantly agreed to it a few days later. He knew where he wanted it to happen and we packed for a day hike and left early the next morning.

As we descended the barren hills, we alternated between animated conversations and silence. I doubted I could do it and Aaron sensed this. Well into the day, we neared a river, and we could see someone in a distant clearing.

We stopped and Aaron put his hands on my shoulders.

"That person. I'll have to kill people like him so I don't get sick. When I get sick awful things can happen and I don't want them to happen anymore. It's not just my not wanting to face eternity in this world."

I understood. We walked down to the river and the sun actually broke through for a moment. He took off his shoes, handed me a large, sharp hunting knife, and stepped into the shallows, looking up at the sky.

"This was a beautiful world," he said.

We were both ready.

#

Bill Richter is a writer living in San Rafael, CA where he lives with his wife, their child, and their dog. His fiction has appeared in *Catamaran Literary Reader, Typishly, So It Goes, The Ocotillo Review* and *The Kentucky Review*. He has had other work published in the books *Hungry? San Francisco* and *Thirsty? San Francisco.*

Mourning Cloak

by Greg Tebbano

When his wife's water broke, Darren was plucking a caterpillar off the back of his neck. The tingle of so many legs—he mistook it for a premonition. That was when he heard Tiffany's astonished cry from the bedroom. Maybe some bit of incredible news just floated past on her phone. When he got upstairs Tiffany sat in a faint puddle on the unmade bed, smirking like a kid caught wading in a public fountain.

"Better get that bag," she said.

In those last weeks carrying her burden, Tiffany's feet swelled. Darren helped her down the stairs while she cradled "her globe," as they called it. Soon the whole world would emerge from her as a tiny person.

Darren tossed her bag in the bed of the old truck. As he was about to open her door, Tiffany stopped him. In the rolled-down window, two butterflies sat slowly pumping their wings.

"It's red today, isn't it?" she said.

"Christ. I forgot," said Darren. The travel restrictions. But this was an emergency.

Darren got her in the truck and the butterflies wafted from the door. Tiffany watched them ascend, their burgundy wings embers.

The engine turned on the third try. It was his dad's truck. Thirty years earlier, it ferried his own pregnant mother to the hospital. His father only told him the story about a thousand times. He was born in the middle of winter. On that night, there had been a storm.

*

Some said fire, others ice. None said wings. Only gardeners and entomologists knew their name—*nymphalis antiop,* or mourning cloak. A harbinger of spring. Traditionally they'd been known to eat up a nursery. In the beginning, these were the images everyone devoured—row upon row of saplings razed to skeleton.

Darren wasn't a hundred percent on the science. Some incredibly hot summers had jiggered their genes. Now they ate everything. The leaves of anything deciduous. But also silage crops, whole vegetable fields turned to compost. In their gluttony, they would starve humanity. A deserved turn, some said.

*

When their son was conceived, it had already begun. As long as Tiffany carried the baby, both she and Darren shouldered a guilt that kept pace. What world would their boy know? With Darren home on indefinite furlough, the question of whether the baby was a mistake filled their days. They berated themselves about it, polished excuses, talked it into the barren ground, hung on each other's words like cocoons until the sun set and the darkness was surround.

*

The truck came down out of the hills, the river high with three days of rain. The damage was first apparent on stands of trees by the roadside, oak and birch and maple, all of them sheared on the sunlit side, as though by an arborist with an untempered Leatherface streak. Shade would be a memory,

Darren thought.

"I knew it was happening, but—" Tiffany cupped her hands over her mouth.

He understood. She hadn't been out in it—seen the familiar undone, the roads they knew like friends.

They passed a corn field that looked more like a trampled festival grounds. Among the few remaining stalks a lone black bear nosed the ground, its fur loose on its frame. This bear looked up at the truck as they passed, its gaze yellowed, lost. Over its shoulder was a patch of mange and within it, a raw, red eye of skin. Tiffany saw it too.

"Darren—" She was hitting him on the shoulder as when he dozed off during a movie, at a part she didn't want to later explain. "I'm gonna be sick."

He eased the truck to the shoulder. Before he could run to help her she was already on her hands in the sand and weeds. He felt her sobbing.

"I don't want to do this," she said.

"Everything's going to be okay," Darren said. They both said it so often. Who knew how easy it was to become a liar.

Just then a state trooper's Impala came onto the flats, the silent lights approaching faster than he thought possible. One summer, Darren went out to Watkins Glen. It was like that. By the third lap he was convinced gravity wouldn't be enough to keep the cars on the track.

The old truck creaked on its struts as the cruiser rocketed past in the direction they were headed. Darren felt Tiffany shiver as they stood together and brushed the gravel from her bare knees.

*

As they drove, the valley widened. The decimated, sunlit fields seemed victims of a storm, but now it had passed. Even the wreckage glittered with god's promise. *Now it was over. Now they were safe.* The truck shook at the limits of its horsepower.

"We should stop," said Tiffany.

She pulled at his shirtsleeve and nodded at the black line on the horizon. He expected them to come first in streaks, preceded by outliers. But no. They came as a darkening sky.

Darren drove on, under some spell. Both he and Tiffany had seen the videos, but this was something else. A swarm. He still said *swarms*. It was always Tiffany who corrected him. By then, there was no one in the world didn't know the name for a mass of butterflies—a kaleidoscope.

They began to hit the truck like dots of rain. In an imitation of what his own father would have done, Darren braced a hand across the chest of his pregnant wife—the truck barreling into darkness as the wind kicked up and the headlights illuminated, for one impossible instant, a way.

#

Greg Tebbano is employed as a grocery worker and, occasionally, as an artist. His fiction has appeared in *Meridian, Hobart, Maudlin House, Contrary Magazine,* and is forthcoming in *Post Road Magazine.*

Formicaries

by Greg Girvan

Worms inhabit my brain. I know they're in there because they give off an odor like the one I remember from going fishing with my father early mornings just before the sun rose.

The worms come and go at night, using my nostrils and ear canals as passageways. Soon after I fall asleep, they depart, sliding out into darkness like top-secret spies, each one on a different mission to collect information on the ants.

"One day, insects will rule the world," Mr. Niles told our sixth-grade science class.

This was during the week after Easter vacation, and I have been waging war on the ants ever since. Every day after school, I spend my time on the patio using a sharp-pointed stone to drill their heads into the concrete. I pretend the stone is a high-powered rifle to make it interesting. I imagine myself as a sniper and make shooting noises.

Sometimes my mother watches me through the kitchen window as she prepares dinner or washes dishes—debating, no doubt, whether or not to take me back to Dr. Seville, the quack I had to see for six full months after my father died last summer.

My sister thinks I'm whacked, too. She's a year older than me and relishes in telling her friends how I spend all my free time murdering ants. If she knew how many ants would eventually be crawling all over her every night as she slept, I think she'd view my actions differently.

*

Each morning, no matter how far they venture off, no matter how difficult their nightly journey, the worms return. Some mornings, in shallow sleep, I swear I can feel their reentry, their slithery but gentle wriggle back through Eustachian tubes and sinus cavities. A sensation of growing pressure goes with it, a sort of stuffy-head feeling, like I'm getting plugged-up with a cold. When the worms depart, it feels the opposite; as they slip out of my ears and nostrils, there's a release, as if they are oozing out of a toothpaste tube or giving birth to themselves, followed by a suction-pop.

Once safely back inside my head, they communicate to my mind whatever ant conspiracies they have discovered during the night. Throughout the remainder of the day, they stay hidden and rest, nestled in the convoluted furrows of my brain.

No one else knows about the worms. After I crashed my bike into Mr. Daugherty's car last month, not even the X-rays or CT scan I received at the hospital detected them. The doctors found only a mild concussion.

*

Some nights I dream I'm buried deep in dark soil, and the worms pass through me as though I am part of the earth. When I turn my head to either side, I see large formicaries—growing kingdoms, huge underground networks most people don't even realize exist.

Often the dream continues until it reaches a horrific climax, which happens when the ants discover I'm lying there, defenseless. Then, one-by-one, they close in from all sides and begin to feed on me. As it becomes clear I'm nothing but fodder for the new world order, I usually wake up, sweating and half-screaming.

When I envision my father buried in the ground like that, I pray his casket is completely impenetrable—solid, built to last forever. I often worry it might not be sealed tight enough, that thousands of ants might at this very moment be thriving on him.

*

This morning, after one of those dreams, I am awake before dawn. My heart is racing. I already know I won't fall back to sleep, which sucks, because after lunch I have study hall and will certainly crash—which means another detention and another hour taken from my mission.

It strikes me then that a surprise predawn attack could prove enormously successful.

I sneak down the hall into the kitchen and quietly open the door to the garage. The cool damp air smells of the cut grass caked inside the lawnmower. Searching in darkness, I find the flashlight on its shelf and locate the spade shovel and a can of Raid.

The eastern sky has begun to glow white. I head across the backyard, toward the huge anthill behind the rhododendrons. I set the flashlight on the dew-soaked grass, aiming the bright beam over the elongated mound. Then I attack. The ants go berserk, darting helter-skelter in every direction as I dig and chop into their kingdom and spray them with Raid.

I don't realize I've been yelling until my mother comes around the rhododendrons in her bathrobe. "William!" she shouts. "What are you doing?"

Startled, I drop the can. My mother picks up the flashlight and shines it on the hole I've dug. "My God!" she says.

*

My mother makes me sit at the kitchen table and in a concerned, shaky voice, begins asking me questions about what I was doing and why. I try to explain how ants are conquering the earth. But this only upsets her more.

"Remember when you thought bees were taking over the world?" she asks. "How you thought honey was poison?"

"This is different," I say. And that's when I goof by telling her about the worms.

My mother stares at me, stunned. She tries to say something but stammers. Then her lower lip quivers and her eyes well up. "Oh, William," she says, all croaky. She hugs me and starts to cry. "Everything will be okay, baby. Mommy's going to get you help."

When she blabbers on about how Dr. Seville can destroy the worms, I cringe and my entire body starts to shudder. She doesn't understand.

"Without the worms we are doomed!" I scream.

My mother hugs me harder. "Calm down," she says between sobs. "I won't let the ants get us. I promise!"

Outside, the sun has begun rising over our ant-infested backyard.

I break into a cold sweat.

I can feel the worms squirming inside my head.

#

To Catch a Moon

by Tiffany Meuret

The old witch looked upon the empty space where the water had been, now caked in mud and the bodies of the fisherpeople who tried to catch the moon. That slice of town gripped by the fever in which they buried themselves. Each of them clutching their devices—their ladles and pitchforks—against their heartless chests, dead and rotting.

It was night again and the moon was back like a deep sigh of wind. The witch caught glimpses of it in her own reflection, bouncing between her shiny, smiling teeth, baring it predator-like.

"Fools," she said. "It was here all along." But none of them liked the sight of her mouth. It repelled them like darting spider legs, her lips scattering away from her voice in search of reprieve from their heat.

So she picked through the bodies, taking note of how they died—arm in arm, aghast, muddy despair caked in darting streams down their cheeks.

"Fools," she said again. They needn't die. If only they'd listened.

The witch was alone now. The city of the fisherpeople sunk

into surrounding marshland of her ancestors, each home an active sore. No matter—it would be reclaimed as the others had, continuing to sink until it caught on the corpses of the towns before it.

The old witch was alone again. Still. As keeper of the moon and stars, night shaped underneath her watchful gaze.

She marked their graves with lilies, and threw them a coin for the oarsman. "Rest well," she said, leaving the fisherpeople to cower under the points of her teeth, aching for the moon they never stood a chance to receive.

#

Tiffany lives in Phoenix with her husband, children, and two chihuahuas, Zeus and Blue. Find out more about her and her work at www.TiffanyMeuret.com.

ODYSSEY

"There is a time for many words,
and there is also a time for sleep."
– Homer

Toward the Sun

by Aeryn Rudel

We walked toward the sun, orienting ourselves when it was lowest in the sky, figuring that would lead us west. We walked beside dead fields of wilted brown, cracked riverbeds that held only dust and bones, and the scorched concrete monoliths of sunbaked cities.

There were five of us when we set out from Boston, three men and two women. We each carried the weight of lost children and loved ones left drained of moisture and life in houses and apartments little more than heat-scorched tombs. Five strangers brought together by the sun grown red and massive, beginning its death throes billions of years ahead of schedule. Our star faced the end with haughty pride, and refused to give up its bright throne in the sky.

The sun shone nineteen of twenty-four hours when we started our journey. The few hours of darkness offered brief respite from the murderous glare and triple-digit temperatures. Those hours waned the further west we traveled. By the time we passed St. Louis, the sun only sank below the horizon for a scant three hours.

A faint hope the Pacific Ocean would offer sanctuary pushed us on. One of us, Dr. Ephraim Adams, a tall, strangely cheerful man who'd taught environmental science at Boston University, told us it would be simple to set up a desalination process. We'd have all the water we needed. I doubted him because I'd seen the scorched plain of the Atlantic. Maybe there was still water out there in the middle of all that desolation, a once-mighty ocean reduced to a shallow puddle. Not that it mattered; the heat would bake your insides before you'd gone ten miles.

We scavenged water where we could from small reservoirs in toilet tanks or the occasional cache of water bottles, half-evaporated, warm and awful on the tongue. The water ran out in Las Vegas and reduced our number to four. A small, pretty woman named Jolene Hanson simply sat down in the middle of I-15, the heat mirage rising around her in stifling waves. She looked up at me and smiled. "That's it, Sam. I'm done."

No one argued with her. We understood. I looked back once after we'd left. I'll always remember Jolene staring up at the sun, dead sunflowers beside the road nodding toward her like a line of mourners at a funeral.

The next night, Jamal Holbrook lay down with the rest of us in the fleeting, hazy darkness. The gunshot jolted us all awake. We didn't have the strength to bury Jamal, so I took the gun from his stiff hands and we continued on.

It grew cooler in the Sierra Nevadas, and I wondered if maybe that great expanse of dark blue water would greet us when we came down from the mountains. I dared not hope, but Dr. Adams assured us the cooler temperatures meant the ocean still lapped at sandy shores, cold and vast.

We found an overturned Alhambra truck beneath an overpass in Central California that had evaded looters. The relative cool beneath the overpass had preserved two five-gallon jugs of pure water. We sat in the shade and drank our fill, reveling in something like joy or maybe just appreciation for a slight reprieve before the end. Perhaps we should have conserved the water, but if the Pacific was dry, I wanted to die with spit in my mouth rather than the dust I'd breathed for three thousand miles.

In Modesto, California, about ninety miles from the coast, our numbers fell to two. In the empty tomb-like silence of a shopping mall, Rebecca Lucas met her end. We'd been dragging our water behind us in a child's wagon. Foolish, but we'd stopped believing there were any people left, let alone any people who would harm us. When we stopped to rest and drink, the three men who had been following us attacked.

They shot Rebecca while she sat beside the wagon, drinking from her canteen. The bullet went through her and into one of the big Alhambra jugs. It spewed water tinged pink onto the tile floor in a steady gush, and that's all that saved us. Dr. Adams and I ran, abandoning the wagon. Our attackers were more concerned with the water spilling onto the ground than pursuing us, and we escaped.

Thirty miles from the coast, Dr. Adams started talking to himself. Ten more miles and he began to shout long strings of scientific formulae interspersed with peals of high-pitched laughter. I ignored him for as long as I could, and then, when I could take it no longer, I shot him. I shot him because I wanted quiet. I shot him because I knew he'd lied about the ocean in the west. I shot him because I wanted to die alone.

I arrived in the seaside town of Carmel exactly three hundred days from when I'd left Boston. I passed through empty streets that had once moved to the slow rhythm of crashing waves and delighted visitors with the stinging scent of brine. I heard nothing but the wind. I smelled only dust and my own rancid body odor.

When I reached the beach, it was not empty. Others had heard the myth of the Pacific and traveled west. Their bodies lay in the sand, burnt and rotting. I saw gunshot wounds in the bleached skulls of half a dozen. Others, like Jolene Hanson, had sat down and died quietly, their corpses folded around a loved one or perhaps just a surrogate stranger.

The ocean bed stretched on endlessly. A new sea of gray silt, but if I stared long enough at the heat waves rising from over it, I could see blue, hear waves, smell the salt in the air.

I saw footprints heading off into the mirage, dozens and dozens of them. I followed, walking toward the sun, always toward the sun.

#

Aeryn Rudel is a writer from Tacoma, Washington. He is the author of the Acts of War novels published by Privateer Press, and his short fiction has appeared in *On Spec* and *Pseudopod*, among others. His debut flash fiction collection, *Night Walk*, was published by The Molotov Cocktail in 2021. He occasionally offers dubious advice on writing and rejection (mostly rejection) at www.rejectomancy.com or on Twitter @Aeryn_Rudel.

The Bottomless Well

by Alex Sobel

I remember seeing it, like a birthday candle burned beyond the wick. That day, playing on the lawn, the sky became fire in front of me, the air catching, flames spreading across the clouds.

When I dream, it follows me. I jump over fences, slide through alleys, pivot sharply to avoid the fireball, but it always finds me. Sometimes I know I'm dreaming, know I'm safe.

Still, I run.

Mom was obsessively clean, so in the months after Dad died, it was unsettling to see dishes in the sink, beds unmade, dust gathered. For the first time since I could remember, the house looked messy. It looked lived-in.

It was a ship that crashed. Interstellar, origins unknown. I felt like I deserved to know why, but there was no explanation of purpose, no reason given.

I remember walking out of the funeral home, seeing my uncle Brock, his eyes tilted to the sky.

"I told him to come work with me," he said, his voice thick, stringy. "I would have taken care of him. Once a baby brother, always one, you know? Should've been at my office in the Pointe, far away from the crash. Safe. Here."

He didn't look down at me. It was like he was talking to the aliens or the planet they came from or something beyond that. Not to me, not to the fatherless boy who was here on Earth.

The salvage operation was mostly fruitless. They recovered no bodies, just the exterior of the ship and scraps of a calcium-like material that must have functioned like bone. The only evidence was the destruction, the hole it left. And when the clean-up was finished not even six months later, there wasn't even that.

Dad's service was only vaguely religious. I never knew if he believed in heaven or if he thought there was nothing after. It's possible he didn't believe in anything, didn't bother. He was the kind of person who participated in life because it was expected of him. Thanksgivings with extended family, grocery store trips, my tee-ball games. All things someone told him to do, the basic requirements of living. So he obliged.

God was one more thing to deal with, another boss nipping away at his time and money.

There wasn't a eulogy. Sometimes when I watch characters in movies give them, I wonder what I would have said, how I would have summed up a life. My father liked sitcoms and Tigers games. He made his own sausage. He once told me his most prized possession was a fishing rod he and his dad had crafted out of bamboo, told me once it was all he had left of his father.

Nothing I could say would seem like enough.

My favorite author wrote a book about the incident, a fictionalized version of the aliens' journey. In the book, they're desperate, fleeing from a planet without a future. The reason they haven't sent anyone else to Earth is that there's no planet left to send another ship. There's no one left to come. They're peaceful, their intentions pure.

Still, they die anyway.

Mom remarried last year. His name is Harvey. His personality is dry, but friendly. A whole room in his house is devoted to Beatles memorabilia. He's an orthodontist. Whenever he makes a joke, he looks over at Mom to see if she's smiling.

She always is.

They're still searching, trying to trace the ship back to its origin, but it feels distant, like dropping a coin down a bottomless well, falling and falling into the darkness forever. And here we are, all waiting to hear the plop of it hitting the water, living our lives as if it'll happen, as if we just need to wait a little longer.

A few billionaires have sent probes out into space with messages, bits of pop culture. One says, "We come in peace," in a hundred different languages. Another plays "All You Need Is Love" as soon as it's opened. Harvey was excited about that one, texted me a link to an article about it. He's trying to be friends with me. I'm doing my best to let him.

The suit I rented for the wedding was boxy and at least a size too big. It was a hundred degrees out. The woman performing the ceremony pronounced Harvey's last name wrong. Mom and I danced together to Fleetwood Mac.

It was a good day.

Mom's selling the house, moving into Harvey's place. Before the honeymoon, she told me to go to the house, take anything I wanted. "There's nothing there I need," she said, grabbing Harvey's arm, pulling him closer.

The fishing rod was in one of Dad's toolboxes. The reel was rusted, glued right to the bamboo. I delicately wrapped it in the emergency blanket from my trunk, put it on the passenger seat. I didn't have a plan for it, but the important part was that it was coming with me, that I wasn't leaving it behind.

I don't think Dad was a believer, but I still hope there's

something after this. I hope there's a heaven. I hope he got in. I hope he saw me take the fishing rod, preserve that little piece of him. I hope he's proud of me.

Dad was here and then he wasn't. I'll miss him.

If I'd given a eulogy, that's what I would have said.

Driving home from my Mom's house, I thought about the billionaires' space probes, traveling into the darkness. I wondered what it would be like if they found something, if there really was something out there waiting for us. I imagine the possibility of a planet, maybe a ship for the probe to meet, an end to the bottomless well. Maybe one day a probe will be opened, maybe "All You Need Is Love" will get its chance to play.

And just maybe there will be someone there to hear it.

#

Alex Sobel is a nurse who writes when he finds the time (which isn't often). His work has appeared in publications such as *Electric Literature, Dark Matter Magazine,* and *Daily Science Fiction.*

Summer Hand

by Jacquelyn Kraut

The kid got nothing right at first. I tried not to laugh when he slipped on the icy snow, but the fourth time it happened I couldn't help myself. Legs flying up and boots in the air and all.

His name was Al and he was the first kid I'd met since Hu died. Twenty-two and shaggy with long, thin limbs. He reminded me of a rabbit when I first saw him, but then when I got to know him he reminded me of a snowy fox. Industrious, curious, and clever. That, and his hair is already going grey. Thin, wintry stripes streaking back from his temples, looking like the snow the wind pulls off the lake.

He's got things down now. He knocks on our cabin door every morning at seven and eats his breakfast quietly. Barbara and I like to talk in the mornings over our coffee but Al stays quiet, staring out of our window at the expanse of snow and scrub. After breakfast he chops some wood for us and then starts checking the traps. He can do it mostly by himself now, even the one in the river. I can hear him chipping the ice away because everything echoes here.

After he checks the traps, he comes in for lunch. Barbara makes us sandwiches on sourdough and Al talks. Everything he says is of interest to me because, to me, he is from another planet. He grew up in Chicago and went to college and has slept with men and women. He is a communist and an atheist. I find him outlandish.

So I listen to him talk. I listen to his ideas about the world, which emerge from him painfully and carefully. When he talks, he hangs his head over his open hands, looking like he's trying to catch his ideas before they disappear. I feel sorry for him, and I feel grateful that I will be dying soon and do not need to trouble much with the state of the world.

I have never troubled much with it. I've troubled with the Land, and the Creatures, and with myself and my family. Barbara and Hu. I trouble with my traps and hanging up our meats to freeze. Every month, I drive the truck the eighty miles to town and then I have to trouble with a few people, and that always feels like an uncomfortable shock to get over with as soon as possible. A five-pound bag of rice, five-pound bag of beans, any produce that's in to please Barbara, a case or two of beer, and I'm gone. When I pass by the people's houses on my way out and see their trailers and outhouses and piled-up tires and swing sets and outdoor furniture and big bins on the curb, I cringe at all of the things. Things are mistakes.

I like Al because he doesn't have much concern for things. He brought one backpack with him here and as far as I can tell it contained clothes and books only. After lunch, we hike the grounds, check the far traps, and skin anything we find to hang. When that's done he lays in the hammock and reads thick books and writes notes in the margins.

Sometimes we cook dinner over an outdoor fire. We sit there until the stars come out—thousands of them. Barbara unbraids her hair, brushes it, and braids it again. And we talk. Al likes to ask us difficult questions. Sometimes Barbara and I sit quietly, waiting for the other to answer.

He almost feels like one of us now, when we three hang around the fire, full on moose. He sits between us like a kid.

It's the third week he's here when Al surprises me and asks about Hu. I don't say anything for a minute, just look at Barbara, because nothing reminds me of Hu more than her. She was his mother and that lingers on her like a burn.

The Land around us is quiet; I can't see further than ten feet around the fire, than the trees caught up in the light like exposed bones. Al is hanging over his hands again.

"Hu was our boy," Barbara begins. When my wife talks she looks at the sky. "He got swept up in the river when he was twelve."

"The river where we trap?

"Yes."

Al says nothing, just sort of folds in on himself. Barbara and I glance at each other over his head.

"Al?" Barbara says, putting her hand on his knee.

"I am so sorry." His voice wavers.

Barbara keeps patting him and I stay where I am. His emotions don't make me uncomfortable, which surprises me. Again, I feel sorry for him.

"Young man," I say, putting my plate on the log beside me. "It is not your job to carry all the heavy things in the world."

When I was first getting to know him, back when I thought he was a hare, I thought the grief that came off him was personal. I thought he lost someone, like his dad, but when he became the fox I realized I was wrong. He spoke of precarity, of alienation, of warehouses full of rubber ducks. He spoke of camps, of money and tragedy and farce. Always his open hands beneath his mouth, open to catch his grief rising in his throat like bile. It stunned me, this boy burdened, when I have only been concerned with survival.

"How can I not?" he says.

I now see that that's why he came here to work for us. Maybe in Alaska, maybe when he's checking traps and fighting the cold and sleeping under a down blanket with his breath fogging the shed window will he just feel the aches of his body and nothing more. But even here grief pulls us into rivers and the world reaches us in cold echoes.

#

Jacquelyn Kraut is a writer living in Chicago. She is currently working on her first novel.

Following Walls

by Chris Panatier

"Where are we going?" I ask, tumbling into the back seat after my brother with our hastily packed bags.

"Away, Lauren. Somewhere else. It doesn't matter. It's the walls again," says Mom with a shudder. "They're full of wasps."

I can't even roll my eyes before she puts the car into reverse and hits the gas. We shoot out of the driveway like we're running from the law. She jams the shifter down and floors it. I glance at Jacob. He's staring at me. We both turn and look out the back window as the house disappears.

She left the garage door open.

"Mom," I say, making a gentle entreaty. "The garage door–"

"Let them have it. We aren't going back."

"Let who have it? Our lives are in that house," I say, my voice going from diplomatic to angry. "This is the fourth move in like a year."

"And we'll keep moving until they stop following."

She's talking about the wasps. The ones she claims are inside the walls of every house we've ever lived in. She'll swear to hearing them, yet when the bug guy comes, they're miraculously gone. It's gotten worse since dad left, no question about that. He heard things too.

"Am I going to be able to go back to school?" asks Jake, who is in fourth grade. "I just made a new best friend. Brett."

Finding a break in her mania, Mom glances over her shoulder and softens. "Jake, baby. We've crisscrossed the state. It's time to try somewhere else, okay? Higher altitude. Desert. Utah, maybe. I don't think they have as many wasps."

"Utah?" Jake cries.

I barely know where Utah is and I'm a high school junior. The middle-ish? I can't get mad at it, really. It's so bonkers that I actually have to hide my smirk.

We drive for days, stay in motels. Mom spends half the time with her ear to the cheap floral wallpaper that seems standard in motor lodges. When she fails to detect the telltale buzz, she tosses out the idea of becoming vagabonds, wandering from inn to inn, taking advantage of their silent drywall. I know it won't last.

It's early morning when we cross from southern Colorado into Utah's southeastern corner. Mom wasn't wrong, it's high and dry. And there's nothing around. We stop in the first place we come to on Highway 191, a nothing town called Bluff that looks one dust storm away from being scraped from the map. Jake isn't impressed either. Mom, though, has that twinkle in her eye that she gets when she's about to listen to her heart and ignore her head.

"No, Mom," I say. "We just got into the state. Don't you want to check it out?"

We pull into a gas station. She punches her door open and pops out, then trots in. We scramble from the car and follow. Inside, she's sweeping up bags of chips and beef jerky, frozen pizza and a six pack of soda. With a big grin on her face, she dumps it all in front of a clerk. Bemused, he smiles back.

"Do you get wasps here?" she asks. "Hornets? Anything like that?"

The clerk actually looks at me and I shrug. *You're on your own, buddy.*

"Well," he answers. "You're in about the only place in the state outside of Moab where they're pretty controlled. Not a lot of water for them unless you get down by the San Juan, but they don't venture far from the river. Further you go up the hill here," he shoots his thumb at the wall behind him and presumably to the topography outside, "the less chance you'll see them. This everything?"

"It is," says Mom, cheerfully handing over her debit card.

*

Within days, she's signed a lease on a tiny ranch-style place up the hill. I can literally see the roof of the convenience store from my bedroom window. But the guy had been right. No wasps. Mom is sleeping through the night now. Doesn't even listen to the walls anymore. She got a job helping out at a rock shop. I've never seen her happier.

Not me though. The town is a shithole. It won't do. The prospect of being stuck here…it's too much. No.

One afternoon while Mom's got Jake at the shop, I grab the long screwdriver with the red handle—Dad's, the one I always use—from the toolbox in the car and drop it in a paper grocery bag like usual. I walk down the driveway past the gas station, take the underpass beneath 191, and head down a walking trail toward the river.

Up from the water is a shed of some type. I round it and find what I'm looking for on the last corner under an eave. And it's glorious, the size of a sunflower, just loaded with eggs and covered in wasps tending them.

Standing on an overturned bucket, I steady myself. Slow. I remove the screwdriver and open the mouth of the bag good and wide, letting it balance on the palm of my hand a few inches below the nest. Having gotten pretty good at what I do, I don't hesitate.

A quick swipe of the screwdriver breaks the thin stem that holds the nest to the eave, and it drops into the bag. I've rolled it up before the wasps have any idea what has happened.

By the time I reach the house, the bag is humming like a hair trimmer turned to eleven, the vibrating paper an amplifier for the wasps' cage-rage. "Oh, I get it," I mutter, setting them into an empty junction box embedded in the outer wall of the house—just behind Mom's headboard.

#

Chris lives in Dallas, Texas, with his wife, daughter, and a fluctuating herd of animals resembling dogs (one is almost certainly a goat). He writes short stories and novels, "plays" the drums, and illustrates covers for metal bands and books.

Any Other Way

by Alex Sobel

"If we're going to do it, it has to be now," David says.

He's nineteen, we've been lucky for a year.

It could happen any time.

*

You can tell when one of the attacks is over when the screaming ends, the clenching. It used to keep me awake at night, but like everything else, it fades, blends at the edges, becomes part of everything.

"Dad, you alright?" David asks when we go downstairs. What he means is: are you dead? Did you finally do it?

"Not yet," Dad says. "Is it time?"

David nods. "Before you have another attack."

David's hand steadies, the needle into the bottle, a specific amount into the syringe.

"Who showed you how to do this?" I ask.

He's silent as he plunges the needle into Dad's shoulder.

*

I've tried to do the math, but it never adds up right. How old is Dad? How old was Mom when she eventually succeeded?

I don't even know my own age.

Apparently, Dad resisted for almost a decade before it took over, when David was twelve. It's the only way the timeline comes close to adding up. Still, someone must have helped David tie up Dad, set up his area in the basement when the time came.

Someone must have helped with the cutting.

Someone must have helped stop the bleeding.

*

"Say goodbye," David says as we pack up the car. But there's no one to say it to, we're the last to leave, the last to hold onto something.

*

Dad is out most of the time. Sometimes he slips in, his eyes meeting me, but talking to someone who isn't here.

I realize that I don't know this man, never will.

"Dreams," he says. "Don't make me go. Please." I sit in the back seat with him, needle in hand for when he wakes up enough to make another attempt.

*

I don't catch his face before David bricks the brakes, too late, the impact like a vacuum in my chest. A few children run over to the body. When we get out to see, it's obvious he's gone, that he succeeded.

"I'm so sorry," David says.

They shake their heads, carry the body away, their faces tortured, relieved.

*

I remember David telling me. Dad has it, the urge to end his life, it doesn't affect you until you're about eighteen. I tried counting on my fingers, could feel the tears coming. David pulled me onto his lap.

"Shh, no, it's okay, you're still a kid," he said. "It's a long way away."

*

"Bye bye," Dad says, pupils like buoys dancing on a sea of white.

"Dad," I whisper so I don't wake David. "What's it like? What happens to you?"

"Huh," he says, like he finally understands something, a realization that puts his mind at he ease.

He sleeps, I don't.

Just in case.

*

David's hands have been twitching for a few days. He shakes it off, pumps the steering wheel to hide it. I don't mention it, don't tell him something he already knows.

*

"Damn, he's got no arms or legs?" the kid says, looking through the back window.

"Makes it harder to kill himself," I say.

When David returns with the gas, he looks the kid over. "What do you want?"

"Just looking," he says. "Where you going?"

"North," I say, feeling David's disapproval. "There's a settlement up there, supposedly. With resources."

"Ah, well, good luck there. I'm happy here, got enough food, my wife. All I need."

Later, I ask David about the kid, if he was really married. "They say they are," he says. "And there's no one left to tell them otherwise."

*

"David, are you actually my brother?" I ask him one night, the sun long gone.

The dashboard light hugging his face, I can see he wants to say something profound, something about family, about how adaptable we are, the ways people survive.

"Yes," is all he says.

And even in the dark, I can tell he means it, that the lie contains its own kind of truth.

*

It happens slowly in my head, the breathless moment, clear, determined. We hit the median, driver's side. I wake to a clicking in my jaw. I bite down, feel powder settled between my teeth.

Dad's on top of me, face tucked into my elbow.

Dead.

There's glass in the back of his neck, blood from his head already hardened to brown.

I manage to get the door open and go around to find David in the front seat. I lift his head off the dash. Bloody nose, probably broken, murky bruises powdered around his eye.

But alive.

*

The needle goes right in, the skin soft, willing.

I find another car, the driver long dead, but vehicle intact. There's blood on the passenger side window, petrified into bulky clumps.

I pull up next to David, ease him into the new car.

I want to ask him if he feels any different, if anything's changed, if there's any markers to let him know he isn't the same.

I roll down the window until the blood disappears.

North, I think. Because it's the direction we've picked, because I can't stand still, because I have to go somewhere.

*

When I get there, they take David out of the car, check his vitals, ask me about the sedative I used. There's clearly a procedure for this.

Later, I'm brought before a teenager, one who looks official, a leader here.

"How old are you?" she asks.

A question I don't have an answer for. It could happen any time, the forced change, the downward slope.

She asks again, but all I know is that it'll come for me too, eventually, and I'll be changed, but somehow still be me. And the changed me won't be able to see who I used to be, won't remember the before, won't know there was any other way.

#

Alex Sobel is a nurse who writes when he finds the time (which isn't often). His work has appeared in publications such as *Electric Literature, Dark Matter Magazine,* and *Daily Science Fiction.*

Through a Hole in the Floor

by David Klose

After the fourth time Luna peed on his closet floor, Michael cut up the carpet, using a box cutter from work.

The carpet was hard to cut, and he spent most of his free afternoon strong-arming it. He'd cut a little, pull a little, and repeat. He was overweight and out of shape, and the activity drained him. Luna watched from the other end of the room, her head resting on her paws. When it finally gave, he rolled up the carpet and threw it to the side. It smelled like a mixture of dog piss and the apartment dumpster after a light rain. Sweat pooled at the small of his back, his shirt clinging to his skin.

Beneath the carpet, there was a rectangular piece of plywood, about the length and width of the thick, second-hand TV in his bedroom. He lifted the plywood and discovered a hole—like an uncovered manhole in the street—that led to darkness.

He peered in with the small flashlight he kept on his keychain and saw nothing. He inhaled but smelled nothing. He wondered of the hole's depth. Fingering the insides of his pockets, he fished out loose change. He kept the quarters and the nickel but dropped three pennies into the hole, one at a time. Not a peep.

He grabbed an old hockey stick from the hallway closet and slowly lowered it until he held it by the end of the blade. Then he let go. Again, no sound.

Michael had started bagging groceries at the S&F during his first semester of community college. A way to put petty cash in his pocket, so he could buy cigarettes and alcohol and late-night tacos after the bars closed.

Fifteen years later, and he now managed the frozen section. He restocked the dairy shelves, and most days he ate lunch alone on an upturned milk crate in the walk-in fridge he called his office.

He thought he'd have traveled in his twenties. Now he was nearing thirty-five and was as stationary as ever. He penned a list of places he wanted to visit, in order of preference: Reykjavík, Paris, Moscow, and Seoul. But he assumed that once he started traveling, he wouldn't stop. He believed that there was a question in him, something perpetual, that college couldn't answer, that relationships couldn't answer, and that work couldn't answer. The answer was "out there," and could be found only in the act of leaving one place for another, again and again. But the furthest he got from his hometown of Phoenix, Arizona, was California for the annual family trip to Disneyland.

Michael learned that people will pay to get rid of certain things: a shoebox full of memories; a flannel shirt that reminds you of your ex-husband; dead pet you don't want to bury, but you can't keep around; a gun; a baggie full of cocaine. An average-size body fit down the hole without issue, but wider bodies had to be cut into smaller pieces first.

Michael learned that he could think negative thoughts, make them the center of his focus, then dip his head into the hole.

When he pulled himself out, the thought was gone.

But there were unintended consequences to dipping. He kept a list of things he had unintentionally forgotten: how to tell time; how to use the French press to make coffee; the name of his mother and that his father died of a heart attack two years ago; the colors of the rainbow; how much hot sauce was too much hot sauce on his Mexican food.

These things took time to rediscover, and it was becoming impossible to keep track of the days.

Michael put sticky notes on the appliances and on the food in the fridge, trying to prepare for things he might forget. This is milk, pour it on your cereal. This is the laundry room, where you clean your clothes. He put a note by the hole that read: do not forget to pull yourself back up. On his phone, he found a photo of a dog he did not recognize lying on a dog bed he did not recognize in his living room, which otherwise looked unchanged.

"I had a dog?" he asked aloud because he forgot he lived alone. He looked all over his house for an answer. In the very back of a kitchen cabinet, he found a half-empty bag of dog treats. "I had a dog," he said flatly.

Sometimes Michael forgot who he was and what he did for a living. There was a notebook for this. It explained that in the second bedroom of his home, he had over one hundred thousand dollars in a safe. On the safe was a sticky note with the combination. In the safe, with the money, was a letter explaining how he had so much money and what he had to do to get more. In the margins, there was also the cost of a one-way ticket to Reykjavík, but there were no other clues as to why Iceland of all places or what he had hoped to find there.

He went to the hole in the closet floor and looked down. He wondered of its depth.

#

David Klose is a writer from Phoenix, Arizona. His work has previously appeared in *Foliate Oak Magazine, Hypertext Mag,* and *The Garfield Lake Review.*

The Absorber

by Emily Livingstone

The house groans. Bonnie feels the ghosts panicking, scratching at the walls, unable to leave. Some fight when she comes for them. It's not an easy job. They test kids young, find out who sees ghosts, and make them sponges. Once Bonnie turned fifteen, she was brought, like the others, to haunted locations to absorb the dead.

The country used to be full of vibrant cities. Now, the land is dying, and only small pockets are habitable. The ghosts swarm those.

She finds an old ghost woman in the kitchen. Bonnie likes the ones who keep their human shapes after death. Some become monsters.

Bonnie smiles. "You won't be gone, entirely, if it helps. The others, they're all still here." She taps her head, then opens her palms to take in this ghost.

The woman says, "There's freedom for your heavy load in Spirit City, honey. Ask the attic ghost, if you can catch her. She's been elsewhere."

Bonnie sighs. Most ghosts can't leave the places they haunt. They're dependent on human energy—humans or what they've created—to exist. Those that can act without it are unpredictable.

In the attic, Bonnie holds her hands ready. She's a moving black hole. Her gift grows, even as her body weakens. She's only twenty-one, but her bones ache, and she's perpetually tired.

This ghost has distorted itself. It looks like a scarecrow—big head, blurred face, long body. It reaches for her. Bonnie absorbs its outstretched claws, whispering, "What is Spirit City?"

"A place where ghosts are free," it spits. "What do *you* care, jailer?"

*

After, in the hotel, captive ghosts float through her dreams, whispering.

Bonnie asks them, *What about Spirit City? We could all be free.*

The face of tonight's old woman appears. She confers with the others, and they build Bonnie a mental map from rumors they've heard.

*

Bonnie's never tried to escape, so her keeper isn't suspicious. She takes his keys and leaves.

She stocks up on supplies and drives west, leaving the living behind.

Hours in, she slows the car by a ghost in military uniform.

"Why's a jailer this far west?" he asks.

"I'm looking for Spirit City, to free us."

"Can I come?"

Bonnie puts out her hand to absorb him, then stops. "Get in," she says.

He drifts into the passenger seat.

Could she have taken ghosts with her this way all along? What if, instead of crowding her head, they walked alongside her? But some would never have come, no matter what, and the keepers would have punished her.

*

Bonnie welcomes other ghosts from abandoned cities as she goes west.

There are no plants or animals. No water.

"What do I do when I get there?"

They've heard there's a stone she touches.

"What then?"

No one knows.

Day and night, the ghosts speak. Some crawl into parts of her body. She feels them, inflaming her joints. Eating at her liver. Fraying the neurons. Sponges don't live long.

*

As Bonnie approaches Spirit City, she drives a clown car of ghosts.

No skyscrapers, just a few broken structures and a crumbling road. Ghosts of every description walk, crawl, and float, coming closer.

Bonnie exits the car. Her hitchhikers form a ring around her, and she asks the city ghosts, "Where's the stone?"

They part, forming a path to a massive rock.

Bonnie kneels, pressing her palms against the stone. She gasps as the ghosts spring out with such force that she falls backward.

Hungry spirits come from every side. She's the only living thing for miles. The old woman, free now, stands over Bonnie. The hitchhiker ghosts stand with her. Bonnie rises and opens her palms, the pose of absorption. The starving ghosts cringe back.

"I don't want to do it, but I came here to live."

Slowly, the ghosts press closer, eyes locked on Bonnie. To her horror, they feed on her protectors, causing her friends to flicker and dim.

"Step back," she murmurs to her circle.

"Too many," the old woman grunts. "You'll die."

Bonnie closes her eyes, becoming the black hole. The dead flood into her. A whole world of suffering, loneliness, and injustice spreads beneath her skin.

When Bonnie opens her eyes, there's not a ghost in sight.

Inside her: chaos. A thousand mouths moving. She contains multitudes. She is legion.

"*What now*?" the soldier says in her head.

"An experiment."

Bonnie pulls up her friends in her mind's eye. She touches her fingertip to the stone, and they diffuse out of her.

"And the rest?" the old woman asks, worried.

Bonnie winces. So many fingernails, clawing at the coffin of her body.

"If I let them out, they'll consume you."

Against their protests, Bonnie orders them into the car. They continue west. She envisions the Pacific, blue and promising.

*

Her head aches. Her eyes lose focus and the car swerves. She drives on.

In the hills, her strength runs out.

She crawls from the car.

As she dies, she holds tight to the long chain of ghosts inside her, bringing them along to the next place. She hopes the hitchhikers will make it to the ocean somehow, traveling on her wish for them, but for all she knows, they'll stay on this hilltop, gathered around her bones for eternity, or until civilization spreads this far, and a new absorber comes for them.

#

Emily Livingstone is a writer, teacher, and mom living in Massachusetts and writing strange stories in the dark when the kids are asleep. Her work has been published in *The Molotov Cocktail, X-RAY Literary Magazine, Jellyfish Review,* and others, and has been nominated for a Pushcart Prize and Best Small Fictions.

Island

by Jamie Cooper

When you wash ashore the morning after a lightning bolt split the mast of your little ship and sent your crew screaming into the drink, you wake up facedown on the sand and cough up all the seawater in your belly. You cough up other things too: tiny crabs, seaweed, an old skeleton key. You thank the island for being an island and not the sea.

But the sea is still inside you. You can feel its tides and swells with every movement. Your ears are like the openings of seashells. All you want to do is sleep, so you do. You lie back down in the sand and let the warm tide wash over you. When you wake, the bloated bodies of your shipmates have washed up beside you. Their eyes are as blue and clear as the water and the sky. When you wake again they are gone. It is dark, and you hear whispers.

You must get used to the island whispers. The whispers tell you things. They tell you things about the past and, more importantly, about the future. About your future. On the Island. And the future of the world outside the island. A future you will never see.

You must make your own future here. The whispers tell you that the island will sustain you. That everything you'll ever need is right in front of you.

But later you start to hear new whispers. And they tell you that the other whispers are liars. You try to find where the whispers are coming from. You follow them to the top of a high cliff. When you get there, you can hear them back down below.

You follow the whispers into a cave. Inside the cave you find a man who looks very much like you, but older and bonier and with long dirty hair and a beard all the way to the ground. He walks in circles, muttering to himself. He says that he has been waiting for you for a very long time. He says he always knew you'd come. He says that together you can live on the island forever.

But you know he is a liar. So when he turns around, you pick up a large rock and bash his head in. When you leave the cave, the whispers go quiet. You sit on the shoreline for a very long time, until your lips are cracked and bleeding. You understand that the island wants to be worshiped, so you build a small temple in the sand. You rename the stars and constellations in its honor.

From above, the signal fire resembles a star that has fallen to the Earth. From above, it's impossible to tell that there's someone down there, waiting in all that darkness to be saved.

#

Jamie Cooper is a graduate of the Iowa Writers' Workshop and a recipient of a 2020 Oregon Literary Fellowship. His chapbook, *The Truth About the Sun,* is forthcoming from *Finishing Line Press*. His work has most recently appeared in *Blue Earth Review, Tempered Runes Press, Fractured Lit,* and elsewhere. He lives in Portland, Oregon.

Frequent Flyer

by Maura Yzmore

The gray-haired woman in Economy Class, seat 12C, looks uncomfortable, beads of sweat on her forehead and upper lip. She grabs the in-flight magazine with a tropical island on the cover and fans herself, unaware she could open the air vent. I decide to help. The woman doesn't see me—most people don't—as I slither along the underside of the carry-on luggage compartment. I envelop the air vent, tilt it toward her, and turn it up all the way. She sighs and relaxes into her seat under a refreshing stream of cool air.

A young man with short black curls, seated in 12B, glances up from his book and smiles at the joy on his neighbor's face. He reaches up toward his own air vent and, for a split second, freezes mid-motion. He saw me from the corner of his eye—I am a whiff of green smoke with a face, an apparition—but he will convince himself that it was nothing. He turns up his air and goes back to his book.

My favorite flight attendant, Mary, is working today in Business Class. Her thick, brown hair begs to be released from the shackles of a tight bun. Mary looks so much like my wife did when we first met. I wish I could remember exactly how long ago that was, but time flows so differently now.

I think about my wife a lot. Maybe it's to atone for not thinking about her enough while I lived. I was on this plane, in the Business Class bathroom, deep inside a blonde from Denver whose name now eludes me, when my chest tightened like an angry fist and never relaxed.

Mary serves Scotch on the rocks to a balding man in 4B. It's his third and his tie is loose, as is his tongue. Mary avoids eye contact and deflects his intrusive questions. He pushes a twenty into her palm and closes her fingers around it, then holds her hand between his, a bit too long and a bit too tight. When she finally breaks free and drops the money onto his tray table, he grins like a cartoon tomcat.

I glide down the partition between Economy and Business, over the floor, along his leg and up to his hand, and I wait. When the man in 4B brings the glass to his lips, I push it from the bottom. The mix of ice cubes and brown liquid spills all over his shirt, and he jumps up, swearing. Mary can't help but snicker before she grabs a towel and rushes to help him.

There is commotion in Economy Class. The man in 12B is standing up, waving both arms and calling for help with a desperate, pleading voice.

The woman in 12C has passed out and is tilted toward the aisle. The air from the vent blows at her, yet she is pallid and drenched in sweat.

The Economy flight attendants are in the back, stuck behind the lunch cart. Mary is nearest, so she runs over, brings her ear to the woman's lips. No breathing. She places two fingers on the artery in the woman's neck. No pulse. She yells for a doctor on board. No hands go up.

Mary asks the young man for help, and they work in tandem to lay the woman on the floor. Mary shows him how to compress the chest. He dutifully follows, while she gives mouth-to-mouth. Still no pulse.

Mary gets up, runs through Business Class, and pulls a defibrillator from a closet with a red cross just outside the cockpit. I wish they'd had those on board back when I was flying.

The man from 4B is up and in Mary's way, demanding that she refill his drink. Her voice is low and unyielding when she tells him to sit down, that a woman is dying. He retreats without another word.

Mary is on her knees, charging the defibrillator. She yells at the young man from 12B to take his hands off, places one pad on top and the other on the side of the woman's chest. The body spasms under high voltage. Still no pulse.

The man continues chest compressions while Mary recharges the pads. I am on the floor now, by the unconscious woman's feet.

Three electrical jolts, and still no pulse. Mary's arms go slack. She is giving up.

The man continues with compressions.

I slide along the prostrate woman's side, toward her chest. I easily pass through her floral dress, permeate layers of skin, muscle, and fat, then squeeze in between the ribs.

In the darkness of the chest cavity, a motionless heart.

I wrap myself around it and think of my own, of how I wish someone had been able to give it one more kick. I think of the wife I left behind, of all the tropical islands I saved my frequent-flyer miles to visit someday with her, but never did.

I squeeze hard, the hardest, a stranger's heart at the center of my phantasmal self…

…and I release.

Ba-bum. Ba-bum.

The woman's lungs fill with air and I hurry back out.

"She's breathing!" Mary and the young man exclaim, and throw themselves into each other's arms. When they separate, the look they share is the same look my wife gave me when she pulled away from me, breathless, after our first kiss, long ago.

#

Maura Yzmore is a writer and scientist based in the American Midwest. Her flash can be found in *Flash Fiction Online, The Arcanist, Utopia Science Fiction Magazine,* and elsewhere. She is a member of the HWA. Find out more at maurayzmore.com or on Twitter @MauraYzmore.

Anglers of Cannon Ridge

by Jiksun Cheung

He considered waking his daughter, asleep beside him in the passenger seat, but decided not to. It had been days since they had eaten anything more than a bit of boiled root and precious shavings of salted fish. They were almost at the top of the ridge; it was better to let her sleep.

He drove hard, forgetting for a while the extinction beyond the flood of the headlights and seeing only the crumbling road in front.

The last mile was steep, so he stepped on the clutch and shifted into low gear. The headlights on the old diesel truck faltered and he felt weightless for a breath.

Do the Shroud things feel weightless up there in the clouds?

The truck lurched forward again and he was pushed back into his seat.

He found the pillbox at the top of the ridge, a squat concrete block with narrow loopholes angled toward the sky where the cannons must have protruded from. The pillbox was deserted, the war of attrition lost years ago.

He pulled over and killed the engine.

His daughter was still fast asleep. In the dark, he could almost imagine that her skin was not sickly pale; that it was not the jaundiced complexion of children born after the Shroud, never having felt the warmth of the sun on their backs. He pulled the quilt over her shoulders and brushed a lock of hair from her face.

*

Outside, the wind barreled past, carrying with it that sour, ungodly stench that reminded him of smoldering tires and rotten fish. Ash swirled around in little eddies as he closed the door behind him, careful not to wake her.

Up here on the ridge, the Shroud, those roiling gargantuan thunderheads that blanketed the four corners of the earth, looked close enough to touch.

He saw a lusterless smear above; it wasn't light, he thought, merely a lessening of the dark. It was the noonday sun.

He flipped on the flashlight and climbed onto the back of the truck. The front was taken up by a row of gas tanks. The rest was occupied by a large coil of graphene cable and an equally massive electric winch bolted to the truck bed.

A door creaked and then thumped shut.

"Baba, what are you doing up there?"

"Morning, sleepyhead. Climb up, I'll show you."

He bent over the edge and lifted her as she scrambled up the side.

He showed her how to prep the winch, how to feed the graphene into the rotating spool. He showed her the large fishing hooks in the duffel, pretending to prick himself on one of the points, eliciting from her a flash of concern and then a knowing giggle. He showed her how to thread the graphene through the eye, how to do the loops and secure it with a double overhand knot. She watched, fascinated, as he tied off another two dozen hooks onto the line.

From another bag, he produced a long skin-like material as if he was a magician pulling a handkerchief from a hat.

"What is that, Baba?"

"You'll see."

The idea had come to him a few days after his wife had passed, when the Shroud had already crept across the sky but had not yet suffocated the land. He had spied a ragged kite, untethered, swept into the air by an updraft, taken higher and higher until he could no longer make out its shape. He'd wondered then what the things in the Shroud would think if they saw it.

"Watch this—" he said. He twisted the valve on one of the tanks and the skin began to fill. It expanded limply at first, but grew and grew until he half expected it to burst.

"It's a balloon!" she shouted, hands muffling her ears.

"A weather balloon."

He rigged it to the end of the line just above the hooks.

"Wanna do the next one?"

By the time they were finished, there were a dozen balloons jostling in the air just above their heads like a bouquet of monstrous white eggs.

"You ready?"

She nodded.

They released it together, his hand over hers. Instantly, the balloons launched skyward, pulling the hooks and the line into the air. The spool spun and jittered frenetically as the white circles climbed toward the Shroud buffeted by the winds in a mad, swirling dance.

They followed as far as their eyes could see.

"Come on."

They shut the doors and fastened their seat belts. He turned the key and the engine roared to life.

He looked back at the winch. The line was taut and had drifted to one side. He traced it all the way up and imagined the bouquet of monster eggs bursting through the Shroud, beckoning at the things that lurked within.

Lightning radiated across the sky, and with each flash he saw dark shapes behind the clouds, circling.

The winch groaned, slow and solitary like the creaking of a boat on a lake.

The truck swayed.

They looked at each other.

He wanted to say something but could only mouth the words: "—be okay." She gave him a tight-lipped smile and found his hand.

The truck listed, harder this time. He heard a zipping and saw that the spool was spinning again, letting out the line.

He put his arm in front of her as if he was braking at a red light. The other hand hovered on the winch control, waiting for the moment.

He craned against the windshield and through the faintest of gaps in the Shroud, he caught a glimpse of rippling, glistening skin not of this world.

"Hold on," he whispered. "Just hold on tight."

#

Jiksun Cheung is a short fiction writer from Hong Kong. His work is published in *SmokeLong Quarterly, Wigleaf, Atticus Review*, and elsewhere. He and his wife share their home with two boisterous toddlers and enough playdough to last a lifetime. Find him on Twitter @JiksunCheung and jiksun.com.

www.themolotovcocktail.com

Made in the USA
Middletown, DE
02 February 2022